Light on Snow

ALSO BY ANITA SHREVE

All He Ever Wanted
Sea Glass
The Last Time They Met
Fortune's Rocks
The Pilot's Wife
The Weight of Water
Resistance
Where or When
Strange Fits of Passion
Eden Close

Light on Snow

A NOVEL

Anita Shreve

LITTLE, BROWN AND COMPANY
NEW YORK   BOSTON

Little, Brown and Company
Time Warner Book Group
1271 Avenue of the Americas, New York, NY 10020

ISBN 0-7394-5748-9

Printed in the United States of America

for my mother

Light on Snow

Beyond the window of my father's shop, midwinter light skims the snow. My father stands, straightening his back.

"How was school?" he asks.

"Good," I say.

He puts his sander down and reaches for his jacket on a hook. I run my hand along the surface of the table. The wood is floury with dust, but satin underneath.

"You ready?" he asks.

"I'm ready," I say.

My father and I leave his workshop in the barn and walk out into the cold. The air, dry and still, hurts my nose as I breathe. We lace up our snowshoes and bang them hard against the crust. A rust color is on the bark, and the sun is making purple shadows behind the trees. From time to time the light sends up a sheen of pocked glass.

We move at a good clip, dodging pine boughs, occasionally catching a shower on the back of the neck. My father says, "I feel like a dog let out to exercise at the end of the day."

The stillness of the forest is always a surprise, as if an audience had quieted for a performance. Beneath the hush I can hear the rustle of dead leaves, the snap of a twig, a brook running under a skin of ice. Beyond the woods there's the hollow road-whine of a truck on Route 89, the drone of a plane headed into Lebanon. We follow a path that is familiar, that will end at a stone wall near the summit. The wall, square on three sides, once bordered a farmer's property. The house and barn are gone, and only the foundations remain. When we reach the wall, my father will sometimes sit on it and have a cigarette.

I am twelve on this mid-December afternoon (though I am thirty now), and I don't know yet that puberty is just around the corner, or that the relentless narcissism of a teenage girl will make walking in the woods with my father just about the last thing I'll want to do on any given day after school. Taking a hike together is a habit my father and I have grown into. My father spends too many hours bent to his work, and I know he needs to get outside.

After the table is finished, my father will put it in the front room with the other furniture he has made. Fourteen pieces in two years isn't much of an output, but he's had to teach himself from books. What he can't learn from manuals, he asks a man called Sweetser down at the hardware store. My father's furniture is simple and rudimentary, and that is fine with him. It has a decent line and a passable finish, though none of that matters. What matters is that the work keeps him busy and is unlike anything he has ever done before.

A branch snaps and scratches my cheek. The sun sets. We have maybe twenty minutes left of decent light. The route back to the house is easy all the way down and can be done in less than ten. We still have time to reach the wall.

I hear the first cry then, and I think it is a cat. I stop under a canopy of pine and listen, and there it is again. A rhythmic cry, a wail.

"Dad," I say.

I take a step toward the sound, but as abruptly as it began, it ends. Behind me snow falls with a muted thump onto the crust.

"A cat," my father says.

We begin the steep climb up the hill. My feet feel heavy at the ends of my legs. When we reach the summit, my father will judge the light, and if there's time he'll sit on the stone wall and see if he can make out our house — a smidgen of yellow through the trees. "*There,*" he will say to me, pointing down the hill, "can you see it now?"

My father has lost the weight of a once sedentary man.

His jeans are threadbare in the thighs and tinged with the rusty fur of sawdust. At best he shaves only every other day. His parka is beige, stained with spots of oil and grease and pine pitch. He cuts his hair himself, and his blue eyes are always a surprise.

I follow his tracks and pride myself that I no longer have any trouble keeping up with him. Over his shoulder he tosses me a Werther's candy, and I catch it on the fly. I pull off my mittens, tuck them under my arm, and begin to unwrap the cellophane. As I do I hear the distant thunk of a car door shutting.

We listen to the sound of an engine revving. It seems to come from the direction of a motel on the northeast side of the hill. The entrance to the motel is further out of town than the road that leads to our house, and we seldom have a reason to drive by it. Still, I know it is there, and I sometimes see it through the trees on our walks — a low, red-shingled building that does a decent business in the ski season.

I hear a third cry then — heartbreaking, beseeching, winding down to shuddering.

"Hey!" my father calls.

In his snowshoes he begins to run as best he can in the direction of the cry. Every dozen steps he stops, letting the sound guide him. I follow, and the sky darkens as we go. He takes a flashlight from his pocket and switches it on.

"Dad," I say, panic rising in my chest.

The beam of light jiggles on the snow as he runs. My father begins to sweep the flashlight in an arc, back and forth, side to side. The moon lifts off the horizon, a companion in our search.

"Anybody there?" he calls out.

We move laterally around the base of the slope. The flashlight flickers off and my father shakes it to reconnect the batteries. It slips out of his glove and falls into a soft pocket of snow beside a tree, making an eerie cone of light beneath the crust. He bends to pick it up, and as he raises himself, the light catches on a patch of blue plaid through the trees.

"Hello!" he calls.

The woods are silent, mocking him, as if this were a game.

My father waves the flashlight back and forth. I'm wondering if we shouldn't turn around and head back to the house. It's dangerous in the woods at night; it's too easy to get lost. My father makes another pass with the flashlight, and then another, and it seems he has to make twenty passes before he catches again the patch of blue plaid.

There's a sleeping bag in the snow, a corner of flannel turned over at its opening.

"Stay here," my father says.

I watch my father run forward in his showshoes, the way one sometimes does in dreams — unable to make the legs move fast enough. He crouches for better leverage and keeps a steady bead on the bag. When he reaches the plaid flannel, he tears it open. I hear him make a sound unlike any I have ever heard before. He falls to his knees in the snow.

"Dad!" I shout, already running toward him.

My arms are flailing, and it feels as though someone is pushing against my chest. My hat falls off, but I keep on clumping through the snow. I am breathing hard when I reach him, and he doesn't tell me to go away. I look down at the sleeping bag.

A small face gazes up at me, the eyes wide despite their many folds. The spiky black hair is gelled with birth matter. The baby is wrapped in a bloody towel, and its lips are blue.

My father bends his cheek to the tiny mouth. I know enough not to make a sound.

With one swift movement he gathers up the icy sleeping bag, presses it close to him, and stands. But the material is cheap and slippery, and he can't get a decent grip.

I hold my arms out to catch the baby.

He kneels again in the snow. He sets his bundle down, unzips his jacket, and tears open his flannel shirt, the buttons popping as he goes. He unwraps the infant from the bloody towel. Six inches of something I will later learn is cord hang from the baby's navel. My father puts the child close to his skin, holding the head upright in the palm of one hand. Without even knowing that I've looked, I understand the infant is a girl.

My father staggers to his feet. He wraps his flannel shirt and parka around the child, folding the jacket tight with his arms. He shifts his bundle to make a closed package.

"Nicky," my father says.

I look up at him.

"Hold on to my jacket if you need to," he says, "but don't let yourself get more than a foot or two behind me."

I grab the edge of his parka.

"Keep your head down and watch my feet."

We move by the smell of smoke. Sometimes we have the scent, and sometimes we don't. I can see the silhouettes of trees, but not their branches.

"Hang in there," my father says, but I don't know if it is to me or to the infant against his chest that he is speaking.

We half slide, half run down the long hill, my thighs burning with the strain. My father lost the flashlight when he left the sleeping bag in the snow, and there isn't time to go back for it. We move through the trees, and the boughs scratch my face. My hair and neck are soaked from melted snow that freezes again on my forehead. From time to time I feel a rising fear: We are lost, and we won't get the baby out in time. She will die in my father's arms. No, no, I tell myself, we won't let that happen. If we miss the house, we'll eventually hit the highway. We have to.

I see the light from a lamp in my father's workshop. "Dad, look," I say.

The last hundred yards seems the longest distance I have ever run in my life. I open the door and brace it for my father. We wear our snowshoes into the barn, the bamboo and gut slapping as we make our way to the woodstove. My father sits in a chair. He opens his jacket and looks down at the tiny face. The baby's eyes are closed, the lips still bluish. He puts the back of his hand to the mouth, and from the way he closes his eyes I can tell that she's breathing.

I unlace my snowshoes and then undo my father's.

"An ambulance won't make it up the hill," my father says. Holding the child against his skin, he stands. "Come with me."

We move out the barn door, along the passageway to the house, and into the back hallway. My father takes the stairs two at a time and turns into his bedroom. Clothes litter the floor, and a fan of magazines is on the bed. I hardly ever go into my father's bedroom. He snatches up a sweater but tosses it away because of the roughness of the yarn. He gathers up a flannel shirt and realizes that it hasn't yet been washed. In the corner is a blue plastic laundry basket that my father and I take to the Laundromat every week or so. Betweentimes he uses it as a kind of bureau drawer.

"Hand me that," he says, pointing.

With one arm, he sweeps the magazines from the bed. I set the laundry basket on the mattress. He takes the baby out, wraps her in two clean flannel shirts, front to back, the small face above the folds. He makes a nest of sheets in the basket, and then he lays the infant gently in.

"Okay then," he says to steady himself. "Okay now."

I climb into the truck. My father sets the basket on my lap.

"You all right?" he asks.

I nod, knowing that no other answer is at all possible.

My father gets into the truck and puts the key into the ignition. I know he's praying that the engine will start. It catches the first try only half the time in winter. The engine coughs, and he coaxes it to a whine. I'm afraid to look at the infant in the plastic basket, afraid I won't see the tiny puffs of breath in the frigid air, mimicking my own.

My father drives as fast as he dares. I grit my teeth in the ruts. The frozen lane is ridged up from the early snows and thaws of the fall. In the spring, before the town comes by to grade it, the road will be nearly impassable. Last spring, during a two-week melt, I had to stay at my friend Jo's house so that I could go to school. My father, who had taken great pains to be alone, finally walked into town one day, both to see his daughter and to break his cabin fever.

Marion, who tends the register at Remy's, tried to bring him home in her Isuzu, but she couldn't make it past the first bend. My father had to walk the rest of the distance, and his calf muscles ached for days.

The baby snorts and startles me. She gives a wail, and even in the weak light from the dashboard, I can see the angry red of her skin. My father puts his hand out to touch her. "Atta girl," he whispers in the dark.

He keeps his hand lightly on the soft mound of flannel shirts. I wonder if the motion of soothing Clara is coming back to him now and hurting his chest. The road down the hill seems longer than I remembered it. I hope the baby will cry all the way to Mercy.

My father guns the engine when he hits the pavement, and the truck fishtails from ice in the treads. He pushes the speedometer as high as he can without losing control. We pass the Mobil station and the bank and the one-room elementary school from which I graduated just the year before. I wonder if my father will stop at Remy's and hand the baby over to Marion, who could call for an ambulance. But my father bypasses the store, because stopping will only delay what he's already doing — delivering the infant to someone who will know what to do with her.

We drive past the small village green that is used as a skating rink in winter. In the middle is a flagpole with a spotlight on it.

Who left the baby in the sleeping bag?

My father turns at the sign for Mercy. The driveway to the hospital is lined with yellow lights, and I can see the baby, scrunching her face, ugly now. But I remember the eyes looking up at me in the woods — dark eyes, still and watchful. My father pulls up to Emergency and leans on the horn.

The door on my side swings open, and a security guard in uniform pushes his face into the truck.

"What's the horn for?" he asks.

I watch the baby disappear behind massive automatic doors. My father puts his head back and closes his eyes. When we hear the distant wail of a siren, he sits up. He wipes his nose on the sleeve of his jacket. How long has he been crying? He turns the key in the ignition, stripping the starter because the motor is already on. He drives as if he were new at the wheel, following signs to the parking lot. When we get out of the car, he looks down, only then realizing that his shirt is still unbuttoned beneath his jacket.

At the curb in front of the emergency entrance, my father hesitates.

"Dad?"

He puts his arm around my shoulder and we walk toward the entrance, our boots coasting on the salt pellets.

The beige-and-mint entryway is empty, and there seems

to be a lot of metal. I squint in the overbright lights that flicker like a strobe. I wonder where the baby is and where we should go. My father follows signs for Triage, each step forward on the tiles an effort. We don't belong in here. No one does.

We turn a corner and see a small room in which a half-dozen people sit on plastic chairs attached to the walls. A woman in jeans and a sweater is pacing, her yellow hair still bearing the imprint of her rollers. She seems impatient, annoyed with a sullen boy who might be her son. He sits in his plastic chair, his coat still on, his chin besieged with angry pimples. I think I see the reason for the visit in the way he cradles his right hand: a finger? a wrist? My father walks toward the Triage window and stands at its opening while a woman speaks into a telephone and ignores him.

I put my hands into the pockets of my jacket and look down the hallway. Somewhere there is a room and a cot and a doctor working on a baby. Is she still alive? The receptionist taps on the window to get my father's attention.

"I brought in a baby," my father says. "I found her in the woods."

The woman is silent a moment. "You found a baby?" she asks.

"Yes," he says.

She writes something on a pad of paper. "Does the child have injuries?" she asks.

"I don't know."

"Are you the father?"

"No," he says. "I found her in the woods. I'm not a relative. I have no idea who she is."

The receptionist studies him again, and I know what she is seeing: a tallish man in a stained beige parka; forty, maybe forty-five; a three-day growth of beard; dark brown hair with a sheen of gray; sharp vertical lines between the brows. My father probably hasn't had a shower, I realize, since breakfast the day before yesterday.

"Your name?"

"Robert Dillon."

She writes quickly, in red ink. "Address?"

"Bott Hill."

"You have insurance?"

"I have insurance personally," my father says.

"May I see your card?" she asks.

My father feels in all his pockets, and then he stops. "I don't have my wallet with me," he says. "I left it on a shelf in the back hallway."

"No driver's license?"

"No," my father says.

The receptionist's face goes still. She sets her pen down and folds her hands together in a slow, controlled manner, as if she were afraid of sudden movement. "Take a seat," she says. "Someone will be right with you."

I sit next to a man with a doughy face who coughs quietly into the collar of a quilted parka the color of weeds. The light is harsh and unflattering, making the elderly look nearly dead and even the children blotchy with imperfections. After a time — twenty minutes? half an hour? — a young doctor in a white coat steps into the room, a mask loose around his neck, a stethoscope anchored in a breast pocket. Behind him is a uniformed policeman.

"Mr. Dillon?" the doctor asks.

My father stands and meets the men in the center of the room. I get up and follow. The doctor is pale and blond and looks too young to be a doctor. "Are you the man who found the infant?" he asks.

"Yes," my father says.

"I'm Dr. Gibson, and this is Chief Boyd."

Chief Boyd, one of only two police officers in the town of Shepherd, is, I know, Timmy Boyd's father. They are both overweight and have the same rectangular black eyebrows. Chief Boyd pulls a notebook and a short pencil from a uniform pocket.

"Is she all right?" my father asks the doctor.

"She'll lose a finger, possibly some toes," the doctor answers, rubbing his forehead. "And her lungs may be compromised. It's too soon to tell."

"Where'd you find her?" the chief asks my father.

"In the woods behind my house."

"On the ground?"

"In a sleeping bag. She was wrapped inside a towel inside the bag."

"Where are the towel and bag now?" Chief Boyd asks, licking the tip of his pencil, a gesture I've seen my grandmother make when composing her shopping lists. He speaks like most of the New Hampshire natives do — with broad *a*'s, no *r*'s, and a slight rhythm to the sentences.

"In the woods. I left them there."

"You live on Bott Hill, right?"

"Yes."

"I've seen you around," Chief Boyd says. "In Sweetser's."

"I think it was near the motel up there," my father says. "I can't remember the name."

The chief turns away from my father and speaks into a radio he has clipped to his shoulder. I study the paraphernalia attached to his uniform.

"How long was she there?" the doctor asks my father.

"I don't know," my father says.

I have then an image of the baby still in the snow in the dark. I make a sound. My father puts his hand on my shoulder.

"Tell me how you found her," Chief Boyd says to my father.

"My daughter and I were taking a walk, and we heard these cries. We didn't know what it was at first. We thought it might be a cat. And then it sounded human."

"Did you see anything? Anyone near the baby?"

"We heard a car door shutting. Then an engine starting up," my father says.

There's a squawk on Chief Boyd's radio. He speaks into his shoulder. He seems agitated, and he turns away from us. I hear him say *twenty-eight years' experience* and *he's here.*

I hear him swear under his breath.

He turns back to us and puts away his notebook and pencil. He takes a long time doing this. "Is there somewhere I can put Mr. Dillon?" the chief asks the doctor. "I've got a detective from the state police major crimes unit coming up from Concord."

The doctor pinches the bridge of his nose. His eyes are pink-rimmed with fatigue. "He can sit in the staff lounge," the doctor says.

"I can run the girl home," Chief Boyd says as if I'm not even there. "I'm headed that way anyway."

I lean into my father. "I want to stay with *you,*" I whisper.

My father examines my face. "She'll stay with me," he says.

We follow the doctor to a lunchroom not far from the waiting room. Inside are tall metal lockers, a pair of cross-country skis propped in a corner, a pile of jackets on a Formica table against the wall. I sit at another table and study the vending machines. I realize that I'm hungry. I remember that my father doesn't have his wallet.

I think about the baby losing her finger and possibly some toes. I wonder if she'll have a handicap. Will she have trouble learning to walk without her toes? Will she be able to play basketball without a finger?

"I can call Jo's mother," my father says. "She'll come get you."

I shake my head.

"I could pick you up after this is all over," he adds.

"I'm fine," I say, not mentioning my hunger, a fact that is sure to get me sent to Jo's. "Will the baby be all right?" I ask.

"We'll have to see," my father says.

"Dad?"

"What?"

"It was weird, wasn't it?"

"Yes, it was."

I shift in my seat and sit on my hands. "Scary, too," I say.

"A bit."

My father takes his cigarettes out of his jacket pocket but then thinks better of it.

"Who do you think left her there?" I ask.

He rubs the stubble on his chin. "I have no idea," he says.

"Do you think they'll give her to us?"

My father seems surprised by the question. "The baby isn't ours to have," he says carefully.

"But we found her," I say.

My father bends forward and folds his hands together between his knees. "We found her, but she doesn't belong to us. They'll try to find the mother."

"The mother doesn't want her," I protest.

"We don't know that for sure," my father says.

I shake my head with all the certainty of a twelve-year-old. "*Of course* we know for sure," I say. "What mother would leave her baby to die in the snow? I'm hungry."

My father pulls a Werther's out of his parka and slides it across the table.

"What will happen to the baby?" I ask, unwrapping the cellophane.

"I'm not exactly sure. We can ask the doctor."

I stick the candy into my mouth and tuck it into my cheek. "But Dad, let's say they let us have the baby. Would you take her?"

My father unwraps his own candy. He balls the cellophane and slips it into his pocket. "No, Nicky," he says, "I would not."

The minutes pass. A half hour passes. I ask my father for another candy. Overhead, on a TV screen, a newsreader announces budget cuts. Three teenagers from White River Junction have been arraigned following an attempted robbery. A storm system is moving in. I study the weather map and then glance at the clock: six-ten.

I get up and walk around the room. There isn't very far

to go. At the end of the row of lockers is a mirror the size of a book. My mouth protrudes because of my braces. I try not to smile, but sometimes I can't help myself. I have smooth skin, not a pimple in sight. I have my mother's brown eyes and wavy hair, which at the moment is kinked up on top of my head. I try to straighten it out with my fingers.

A man in a navy overcoat and a red scarf enters the room without knocking, and I guess that he is another doctor. He unwinds his scarf and lays it over a chair. I can see that my father wants to unzip his jacket, but he can't. He has no buttons on his shirt.

The man takes off his coat and sets it down on top of the scarf. He rubs the palms of his hands together as if anticipating a good time. He has on a black cabled sweater and a blazer, and his face is gravelly with acne scars. To the right of his chin is an extra flap of skin, as if he'd been in a car accident or a knife fight.

"Robert Dillon?" the man asks.

I am surprised that this other doctor knows my father's name, and then I realize he isn't a doctor at all. I sit up straighter in my seat. My father nods.

"George Warren," the man says. "Call me Warren. Want a coffee?"

My father shakes his head. "This is my daughter, Nicky," my father says. Warren holds out his hand and I shake it.

"She was with you when you found the baby?" Warren asks.

My father nods.

"I'm a detective with the state police," Warren says. He takes some change from his pocket and inserts it into the coffee machine. "You told Chief Boyd you found the baby on Bott Hill," he says with his back to my father.

"I did," my father says.

A heavy paper cup tumbles into place. I watch the coffee run from the spigot. Warren picks up the cup and blows over the top.

"The sleeping bag and the towel should still be there," my father adds. "I found her in a sleeping bag."

Warren stirs the coffee with a wooden stick. His hair is gray but his face is young. "Why'd you leave it there?" he asks. "The sleeping bag."

"It was too slippery," my father says. "I was afraid I'd drop the baby."

"How did you carry her?"

"I put her inside my jacket."

Warren's eyes slide to my father's jacket. The detective draws a chair back from the table with the toe of his Timberland boot. He sits down. "Can I see some ID?" he asks.

"I left my wallet at the house," my father says. "I was hurrying, trying to get the baby to the hospital."

"You didn't call the police? An ambulance?"

"We live at the end of a long hilly drive. The town

doesn't maintain it very well. I was afraid an ambulance would get stuck."

Warren eyes my father over the rim of his cup. "Tell me about the sleeping bag," he says.

"It was shiny blue on the outside, plaid on the inside," my father says. "Cheap, like you'd buy at Ames. There was a towel, too. White and bloody."

"You've lived on Bott Hill a long time?" Warren takes another tentative sip of coffee. His eyes are both alert and distant, as if all the important stuff were going on somewhere else.

"Two years."

"Where are you from?"

"I grew up in Indiana, but I came here from New York."

"The city?" Warren says, pulling on an earlobe.

"I worked in the city, but we lived just north of it."

"If it hadn't been for you, Mr. Dillon," Warren says, "we'd have found a couple of bones in the spring."

My father looks at me. I hold my breath. I don't want to think about the bones.

"You hot?" Warren asks my father. "Take off your jacket."

My father shrugs, but anyone can see he's sweating in the overheated room.

"What were you doing when you found the infant?" the detective asks.

"We were taking a walk."

"When?"

My father thinks a minute. What time was it? He no longer wears a watch because he catches it too often in his tools. I glance up at the clock over the door. Six twenty-five. It feels like midnight.

"It was after sunset," my father says. "The sun had just set over the top of the hill. I'd say we found her maybe ten, fifteen minutes after that."

"You were in the woods," Warren says.

"Yes."

"You often go walking in the woods after sunset?"

The detective sets the coffee cup on the table, reaches into the pocket of his overcoat, and takes out a small notebook. He flips it open and makes a notation with a short pencil. I want one of those short pencils.

"On good days," my father says. "I usually quit working around three forty-five or so. We try to take a walk before it gets completely dark."

"You and your daughter."

"Yes."

"How old are you?" the detective asks me.

"Twelve," I say.

"Seventh grade?"

"Yes."

"The Regional?"

I nod.

"You get off the bus what time?"

"Three fifteen," I say.

"It takes another fifteen minutes to walk the rest of the way up the hill," my father adds.

Warren turns back to my father. "How'd you find the baby, Mr. Dillon?"

"With a flashlight. We'd heard her crying. We were looking for her by then. Well, for a baby."

"How long had you been walking?"

A voice over the loudspeaker, asking for Dr. Gibson, interrupts them. I wonder if there's an emergency with the baby. "About thirty minutes," my father says.

"You hear anything unusual?"

"I thought it was a cat at first," my father says. "I heard a car door shutting. And then a car engine being turned on."

"A truck? A sedan?"

"Couldn't tell."

"After you found the infant?"

"No. Before."

"Before or after you heard the first cry?"

"After," my father says. "I remember thinking it must be a man or a woman taking a walk with a baby."

"In the woods? In the winter?"

My father shrugs. "I was headed up the back of Bott Hill. There's a stone wall there. We often make it a kind of destination."

I think of all the times my father has sat on the wall and had a cigarette. Will we ever go there again?

"Could you find it?" Warren asks. "The place where you found the baby?"

"I'm not sure," my father says. "There might be shallow tracks. We were on snowshoes, but the crust was hard. I might be able to show you approximately in the morning."

Detective Warren sits back in his chair. He glances at me and then away. "Mr. Dillon," he says and then pauses. "Do you know anyone who could have given birth to this infant?"

The question startles my father — because of its content, because it has been asked in front of me. "No," he says, the word barely slipping through his lips.

"You married?"

I glance away from my father.

"No," he says.

"Other children?"

A hot wind blows through my chest.

"My daughter and I live alone," my father says.

"So what made you move up here?" the detective asks.

There's a small silence, and I'm wishing I hadn't been allowed to stay in the room. "It seemed like a good idea at the time," I hear my father say.

"Didn't like the pressure?" Warren suggests.

I look up. My father is staring at the skis in the corner. "Something like that," he says.

"What did you do in the city?"

"I worked for an architectural firm."

Warren nods, absorbing the facts. "So what do you do now?" he asks. "Up on Bott Hill?"

"I make furniture," my father says.

"What kind of furniture?"

"Simple stuff. Tables. Chairs."

Behind me, I hear the door of the lounge open. Dr. Gibson enters, peeling off his white coat as he does so. He tosses it into a bin in the corner. He nods a hello to the detective. Either the two know each other, I am thinking, or they spoke before the detective came into the lunch-room. "I'm off now," the doctor says, clearly exhausted.

"How's the baby?" my father asks.

"Better," Dr. Gibson says. "She's stabilizing."

"Could I see her?" my father asks.

Dr. Gibson takes a yellow-and-black parka out of a locker. "She's asleep in the ICU," he says.

I see a look pass between the detective and the doctor. The doctor checks his watch.

"Okay," Gibson says, "a quick peek. Can't see the harm in that."

We follow Dr. Gibson through a series of corridors, all painted the same dispiriting mint and beige. The detective falls behind, and I imagine him studying my father and me as we walk.

The pediatric ICU has been built in the shape of a

wheel, with the nurses' station the hub and each patient room a spoke. I pass parents sitting in plastic chairs, staring at dials and flickering red lights. I am waiting for someone to start screaming.

Dr. Gibson motions us into a room that seems enormous compared with the tiny infant in the plastic box. He gives us masks and tells us to hold them over our mouths.

"I thought she'd be in the nursery," my father says through the blue paper.

"Once the infant has been outside of the hospital, she can't go back into the nursery. Might infect the other infants," the doctor explains. He leans over the cot, adjusts a tube, and examines a screen.

The baby lies inside a heated Plexiglas case. A bandaged hand and foot stick out doll-like from the scrawny body. The hair, black and feathery, covers the wrinkled scalp like a bird's crown. She makes delicate sucking motions as we watch.

I want to put my cheek close to the baby's mouth and feel the warm breath against my skin. Finding her might be the single most important thing my father and I have ever done.

"What will happen to her?" my father asks.

"The Division of Youth Services and Families will take care of her," Dr. Gibson says.

"And then what?"

"Foster care. Adoption if she's lucky."

The four of us go down the elevator in silence. I realize that my father stinks. When we step off, Dr. Gibson puts out his hand to my father. "I'm in the back," he says. "I'm glad you found her, Mr. Dillon."

My father shakes the doctor's hand. "I'd like to call you tomorrow," he says. "To see how she is."

"I'm on all day," Dr. Gibson says. He hands my father a card, and we watch him walk away.

"Where's your car?" Detective Warren asks my father.

My father has to think a minute. "In the front lot," he says.

"I'd like you to come for a ride with me," Warren says. "I want you to take a look at something."

"My daughter's tired," my father says.

"We can leave her here," the detective says. "Pick her up when I drop you off. This won't take long."

"No, Dad," I say quickly.

The detective opens his mouth to speak, but my father cuts him off. "She'll come with us," my father says.

Warren drives a red Jeep, which seems an odd choice for a state policeman. I decide he probably doesn't do too much undercover work. Maybe he needs the truck for chasing criminals on back roads.

"You'll have to give me directions," Warren says. "I don't have much call to come up here."

"To where?" my father asks.

"To the motel," Warren says.

We pass through the small town of Shepherd, New Hampshire, named after Asa Henry Shepherd, a farmer who came up from Connecticut to till the land in 1763. In the local phone book there are over thirty Shepherds listed.

"We're getting some weather tomorrow," Warren says. "Ice, according to the radio. I hate ice."

My father says nothing. It's freezing in the Jeep. I'm

sitting in back. The detective drives with his coat open, the red scarf loose around his neck.

"Black ice is the worst," Warren says. "Two years ago there was this family from North Carolina, coming off the exit ramp to Grantham. They were up skiing, had no clue about black ice. The Chevy they were in went airborne."

I watch the rhythm of my father's frozen breaths.

"A couple checked in to the motel over by you," Warren says. "The owner gave a description of the man but says she didn't see the woman. Male, Caucasian, five-eleven, twenty, twenty-one, black wavy hair, wearing a navy pea-coat. She thinks he was driving a Volvo, six, seven years old. They're supposed to get a plate number, but she didn't."

"A Volvo?" my father asks, surprised.

The detective bypasses our road, heading east toward the drive that will lead to the motel. The headlights provide small glimpses into the forest, the same woods that border our property. Through the windshield I can see a puzzling glow in the night sky, as if there were a small city waiting for us at the top of the hill.

Warren drives with a heavy foot. My father has never liked being a passenger, hasn't been one in years. I can smell the detective in front of me — a mixture of wet wool and coffee, with a faint overlay of spearmint.

"Turn here," my father says.

Warren makes a turn onto a paved driveway that runs

up a short hill to a low red-shingled motel. There are two cruisers and three other cars in the parking lot. Behind the motel the woods are lit with a series of powerful spot-lights.

Warren gets out of the Jeep and beckons to my father to join him.

"You stay here," my father says to me.

"I want to come," I say.

"I'll be right back," he says.

The door to a motel room is open, and I can see two uniformed policemen inside, one of whom is Chief Boyd. My father follows the detective across the lot.

I draw up my knees and wrap my arms around them. The window next to me is smeary, but I can see my father stepping over the threshold and into the lighted room. I don't understand why I've been left alone in the car. What if the person who left the baby to die is still around?

I lean to one side and let my weight topple me onto the cushion so that I am lying on the backseat in a fetal posi-tion. I am in a detective's car. A small jolt of something like excitement mixed with fear tingles at the back of my neck.

I examine the floor of the Jeep in the light from the parking lot. There's an empty Coke can on its side, a used tissue, and several scattered coins. In the pocket of the seat back, there's an atlas and a tape cassette. And what's this? I reach my hand out and touch a Snickers bar, unopened. I pull my hand back. There's a long metal object that might be a tool tucked under the passenger seat. Other than that, the Jeep is fairly clean, not like the cab of my father's truck, which is covered with rags, pieces of wood, sawdust, tools, jackets, and socks. It smells, too — like old apples. My father swears that there aren't any apples in the truck, that he's searched all through it, but I am certain there's at least one rotten one back there somewhere.

I let myself cry for a minute. It feels good, though I have nothing but my sleeve to wipe my nose on. I remember the way my father cried in the parking lot. He seemed not to know I was even there.

My father and I saved a person's life. I'll be a celebrity at school in the morning. I hope my father doesn't tell me not to talk about it. I wonder if I'll be in the newspapers. My teeth begin to chatter, and maybe I help them along a bit. I think about our walk, about finding the baby in the woods, about the way my father fell to his knees. I wonder if being dangerously chilled is reason enough to get out of the car and go inside.

I sit up and peer out the window, which has steamed up a bit. How long has my father been gone? My fingers are cold. What happened to my mittens? I am starving. I haven't eaten anything since school lunch at eleven thirty. I think about the Snickers bar. Will the detective notice if I eat it? And if he notices, will he care? I reach over to the seat back pocket and slip the bar out. I hold it in my lap for a moment, my eye on the door of the motel room. I will have to eat it fast and hide the wrapper. I don't want to get caught with half a candy bar in my mouth.

I tear the wrapper open. The bar is hard from the cold, but the candy is delicious. I eat it as fast as I can, wiping my mouth with my fingers and stuffing the wrapper in the pocket of my jeans. I sit back, slightly breathless.

With shoulders hunched, waiting for a reprimand, I step out of the Jeep and shut the door. I walk across the plowed parking lot. I can hear voices now — the deliberately calm voices of technicians at work. I hesitate on the steps, expecting a bark.

It's a small room and would be depressing even without the bloody sheets or the soiled covers ripped from the bed. The walls are paneled in thin wallboard meant to look like pine. The room has a bureau and a TV and smells heavily of mildew. A bloodied sheet lies just below the lone window, which is open. Through that window I can see the spotlights on the snow.

A technician is working over the bed.

"A woman gave birth in here," Warren is saying.

On a side table is a glass of water, half full. A sock lies on the rug. "There'll be fingerprints," my father says.

"There'll be fingerprints all over the place," Warren says, "but none of them will do us any good unless one of them has a record — which I sincerely doubt." The detective takes a handkerchief from his back pocket and blows his nose. "That tiny girl you found?" he asks. "She started life in this room. And then someone, most likely the father, went out that window there and tried to kill her. No one put that baby in a warm place where she'd be found. No one called in a tip. A man took that infant, minutes old, walked her out into the woods on a December night, temps in the single digits, and laid her naked in a sleeping bag. If you hadn't found her, we'd have come across her, when? March? April? If even then. Most likely a dog would have gotten to her first."

I think about a dog dragging a bone across the snow with its teeth. My father stands near the detective while he confers with a technician. Chief Boyd is leaning against a wall, his lips pressed hard together. From where I'm standing he can't see me. I try to picture what went on in this room. I don't know much about giving birth, but I can feel hysteria in the walls, the wrinkled sheets, the clothes left behind. Did the woman know what the man would do with the infant? The sock is pearl gray, angora maybe, with a cable knit up the side. A woman's sock to judge from the size of it. A technician picks it up and sticks it in a plastic bag.

"In the fifteen years I've been with the state police," Warren says, "I've seen maybe twenty-five cases of abandoned infants. Three months ago, in Lebanon, a woman left an infant in a trash barrel outside her house. She'd broken up with her boyfriend. The baby was dead when we found him. Had Campbell's soup up its nose."

A technician interrupts Warren with a question.

"Last year," Warren continues, "a fourteen-year-old girl threw her baby out a second-story window. She's charged with attempted murder." Warren studies a drinking glass and a plastic bag on the bedside table. "In Newport we found a newborn girl, alive, on a shelf at Ames. Over to Conway they found a newborn boy in a trash bin in the back of a restaurant. The mother was twenty. It was freezing outside. She's charged with attempted murder." The detective squats down to look under the bed. "What else? Oh, in Manchester an eighteen-year-old mother abandoned her baby girl in a park. She left the child in a plastic bag, and two ten-year-old girls discovered the infant when they were biking through the park. Can you imagine? The mother's charged with attempted murder and cruelty." Warren stands. He points under the bed and asks a technician a question. "And listen to this one: Two years ago, a high school senior discovered she was pregnant. She said nothing. She hid it by wearing baggy sweatshirts and pants, hoping all the while that she'd miscarry. But she didn't. In the fall she went off to college. The day before Thanksgiving, after everyone had gone home, she delivered a baby girl on the floor of her dormitory room. She wrapped the infant in a T-shirt and sweater, put her in a plastic grocery bag, and carried her down three flights of stairs. She laid her in a trash bin just outside the dorm."

Warren walks to the window and looks through it.

"But College Girl had a conscience," he says. "She called in an anonymous tip to campus security, and they came and found the baby. Didn't take them long to find the mother either. She pled to endangerment and was sentenced to a year's house arrest."

"How do you know it was a man who did this?" my father asks. "In all the other examples you've just mentioned, it was a woman who abandoned the baby."

"Come with me," Warren says to my father. "I want you to see something."

The two men turn, and as they do they see me just outside the doorway.

My father moves to stand in front of me, as if to block my view of the room, but we both know it's too late: I've seen what there is to see.

"I thought I told you to stay in the car," my father says, both surprised and angry.

"It was cold."

"If I tell you to stay in the car, I mean stay in the car."

"It's all right," Warren says as he slides past my father. "She can come with us."

My father gives me a stony look. He makes me walk in front of him, following the detective around the back of the motel. The snow is deep, and Warren motions for us to step in his slow and precise bootsteps. From a window at the back of the motel, another set of prints stretches into the woods. The lights are so bright I have to put up my hand. Fifty feet from where we stand, two policemen are bent over the snow.

"Bootsteps," Warren says. "They go down two feet in some cases. Size ten and a half. Every twenty feet or so, the guy sank up to his knees in the snow. The tracks go way out, five hundred yards anyway, and then double back. You know how hard that is to do?"

My father says he knows how hard that is to do.

"You could break your leg doing that," Warren says.

My father nods.

"City guy, wouldn't you say?" the detective asks.

"Might be."

"A woman who had just given birth couldn't have done that."

"I don't think so," my father says.

Warren turns toward my father and puts a hand on his shoulder. My father flinches. "Despite the fact that you won't unzip your jacket," the detective says, "that you have blood on your collar, that you're looking a little rough around the edges, and that you live on a deserted road near the motel, you'll be happy to know I don't think you did this."

*   *   *

We ride with Chief Boyd back to town. In the morning everyone will wake to the news. I try to picture again the man and the woman who went to the motel to have a baby and then kill it. Where are they now?

"That's my truck over there," my father says when we reach the hospital parking lot. Chief Boyd drives us to the truck and we get out. "Thanks for the ride," my father says, but Boyd, still tight-lipped, doesn't answer. He peels out of the lot.

We climb up into the truck and my father turns the key. The engine catches on the first try. Two for two. As we wait for the truck to warm up, I look out through a thin layer of frost crystals that shine under the lamplight of the parking lot. Beyond the frost is the front door of the emergency room, and beyond that is a cot in which a newborn girl is trying to start her life.

"You shouldn't have had to hear all that," my father says.

"It's not that," I say.

"What is it?"

"I was just thinking about Clara."

The truck jounces a little as it revs. There's an empty Coke can under my feet that's annoying me. My father guns the engine. He makes a sharp U-turn in the nearly empty lot, and we drive out into the night.

The skid marks were forty feet long. The tractor-trailer pushed the VW along the highway as if it were only so much snow to be plowed out of the way.

My mother died instantly. Clara, who was still alive when the medics got her out of the wreckage, died before the ambulance reached the hospital. It was ten days before Christmas, and my mother had taken the baby to the mall for Christmas shopping. For reasons we will never know — did Clara with her charm or her whining make my mother turn her head, even for an instant? — my mother glided onto the highway in the path of the oncoming truck. The driver, who emerged from the accident with only a dislocated shoulder, said he was traveling at just under sixty-five when the green VW floated across his path.

My father, who had stayed late at his office Christmas party in Manhattan and who was on his second martini when his wife and child were being dragged into oblivion, didn't know about the accident until close to midnight. When he arrived home and found the house empty, he waited an hour or so and then began calling my mother's friends and then the area hospitals and then the police, until finally he received an answer that even weeks later he was unable fully to comprehend. And for months he had the notion that had he not made the telephone call, he never would have heard the terrible news.

That night he drove to the hospital, his own ten-year-old Saab mocking him with its sturdiness. The interns made a grab for him when he went over, and they had to fight to get his tie off so that he could breathe. After he identified my mother, the staff gave him a minute with Clara, who was strangely intact apart from the purple oval bruise to one side of her forehead. The magnitude of the waste was unbearable, Clara's perfect body a unique torment only a jealous god could have devised.

The accident happened on a Friday night when I was sleeping over at Tara Rice's house. Mrs. Rice, who hadn't heard the news, was surprised to see my father at her door so early on a Saturday morning. I was found amidst a scatter of sleeping bags on Tara's floor and told to pack my things. When I walked into the kitchen and saw my father, I knew that something terrible had happened. His face, which had been ordinary enough just the day before, seemed to have been recarved by an inept sculptor, the features rearranged and misaligned. He helped me put my jacket on and walked me to the car. Halfway down the driveway, I started yipping at him, a dog at his heels.

"What, Dad? What's the matter?

"Tell me, Dad. Why do I have to leave?

"What happened, Dad? What happened?"

When we reached the car, I tore my shoulder from his grip and began to run back to the house. Perhaps I thought that by reentering Tara's house I could stop time, that I would never have to hear the unspeakable thing he had come to tell me. He caught me easily and pressed my face into his overcoat. I began to sob before he said a word.

My grief, which I could not articulate beyond a string of helpless words within an open-mouthed wail, showed itself, as the days wore on, in short, violent squalls. I would bend over and pound the floor or rip the covers from my bed. Once I threw a paperweight against my door, cracking it down the center. My father's grief was not as dramatic as mine, but instead was resolute, an entity with weight. He held his body with an awful rigidity, the jaw tight, the back hunched, his elbows on his knees, a posture most easily achieved in a chair at the kitchen table, where water or coffee and occasionally food were brought to him.

For days, my father sat in our house in Westchester, unable to go back to the office. After Christmas vacation, I was made to return to school on the theory that it would distract me. My grandmother came to care for us, but my father didn't like having her there: she reminded him only of happier times when we'd visited her in Indiana in the summer. There we'd spent lazy mornings with Clara in a plastic wading pool and my mother lounging gratefully in a slim black tank suit. In the heat of those afternoons, with my grandmother watching Clara and me, my father and my mother would sometimes slip away to his old childhood bedroom for a nap, and I'd be glad that I'd escaped that dreaded camplike fate.

One day several weeks after the accident, I came home from school on the bus and found my father sitting in the same chair in which I'd left him at breakfast, a wooden chair next to the kitchen table. I was sure that the cup of coffee on the table, with its dark sludge on the bottom, was the same one he'd poured himself at eight a.m. It frightened me to think that all the time I'd been in school — all during math and science and a movie called *Charly* that we'd watched in English class — he'd been sitting in that chair.

In March my father announced that we were moving. When I asked where, he said north. When I asked where in the north, he said he had no idea.

I sit up in the bed and see light at the edges of the curtains. I push the covers away and step onto the cold floorboards.

I raise the shades and put a hand to my eyes. Every twig and late-to-fall leaf is coated with an icy shine. I am giddy with this news. Even in New Hampshire, the school buses won't risk the ice. I turn on the radio and listen to the school closing announcements. Grantham public schools, *closed.* Newport public schools, *closed.* Regional High School, *closed.*

I take a shower, towel off, and dress in jeans and a sweater. I make myself a cup of hot chocolate. Looking for my father, I move, mug in hand, through the rooms of the house, a long, narrow Cape turned sideways with a porch to the west. The house is painted yellow with dark green trim, and in the summer a wild vine grows along the porch railing, creating a kind of trellis. The paint job is ancient and needs to be seen to, and my father plans to tackle it in the summer. Last summer, our second in the house, my father made a small patch of lawn that I was periodically asked to mow. The rest of the property he let go. Where it isn't woods, it's bush and meadow, and on summer evenings we sometimes sit on the porch, my father with a beer and me with a lemonade, and watch birds we can't identify skit along the tips of the overlong grasses. Occasionally, we'll each read a book.

I walk into a front room that runs the width of the house and has two long windows to the south. When my father bought the place, the windows were painted shut, and two tarnished chandeliers hung from the ceiling. The walls were papered in a faded and peeling blue print, and the fireplace was boarded up. My father had picked the house solely for its isolation and the promise of anonymity, but after he spent two weeks sitting in a chair unable to do much but look out a window, he began to meander through the rooms. He decided to strip the house down to its bare bones.

Starting in the front room, he plastered over the ceiling, an ugly expanse that looked like the hardened frosting of a day-old birthday cake. He stripped the walls and painted them white. He bought a sander and refinished the floors, polishing them to a warm honey stain. Sometimes he made me help him; most of the work he did himself. The room has nothing in it now but the pieces of furniture my father has made over the course of the past two years: tables and bookcases and wooden chairs with straight backs and legs. The room is clean and simple and resembles a schoolroom, a look I think my father was unconsciously trying to achieve all along, as if he wished to return to the blank rooms of his childhood. He sometimes uses the space as a showroom when Mr. Sweetser down at the hardware store sends customers his way. The carpentry is a kind of career for my father, though careers were for his previous life, not this one.

In the room that was once a dining room, my father built floor-to-ceiling bookcases and filled them with his books. He put a leather chair, a sofa, two lamps, and a rug in it, and it's the room we sometimes eat and read in. We call it the den. The transformation of rooms into something other than what they were — a parlor into a showroom; a dining room into a den; an old barn into a workshop — has given my father a kind of perverse pleasure. Just beyond the kitchen is a long hallway paneled in cream bead board with a row of sturdy hooks at shoulder height. Off another hallway is a small room that my father didn't know what to do with. He cleaned it up and filled it with boxes that he didn't want to open. As a result the room has become a kind of shrine. Neither of us ever goes inside.

Upstairs there are three bedrooms: one for me, one for my father, and one for my grandmother when she comes to visit.

The kitchen is the one other room my father hasn't tackled. It has a red Formica counter and brown metal-framed sliders out to a redwood deck. Though it is the room that needs the most work, my father goes into the kitchen only to make a quick cup of coffee or a sandwich or a rudimentary dinner for the two of us. We never sit down to a meal there, but instead bring our food to the den when we eat together, or he to his workshop and me to my bedroom when we each eat alone.

We never eat a meal in the kitchen because the kitchen of our previous life was at the heart of our family in New York. The two rooms do not resemble each other much, but the memories of that former kitchen can unravel either one of us in an instant.

The table was always half-covered with magazines and mail. Neither my father nor mother was a fastidious house-keeper, and with Clara just a year old, a case of mild clutter was always turning into serious chaos. My mother made baby food in the Cuisinart on a counter usurped by appliances: a juicer, a blender, a microwave, and a coffee grinder that made a racket like a jackhammer and never failed to wake Clara. Between the table and a hutch was a baby swing, a contraption in which Clara, with drool sliding down her chin, would bounce happily and for long enough that my parents could get a meal on the table. During dinner my father sat with Clara in his lap, introducing her to foods she smashed into her mouth with a fat palm. When she fussed he jiggled her on his knee, and by the time dinner was over, his work shirt would be finger-painted with carrots and gravy and buttered peas.

In my album there's a picture of my mother trying to eat her dinner at the counter while she holds Clara on her hip. Clara has a finger in her mouth and is drooling, and my mother is slightly out of focus, her back to me, as if she might be jouncing Clara up and down to keep her quiet. In the kitchen window just beyond my mother, there's a blinding reflection of a flashbulb. Inside the halo I can just make out my father, beer in hand, his mouth open, about to take a sip. I have no idea why I felt it necessary to take this photo in the middle of dinner, why I thought it important to capture my mother's back or Clara with her finger in her mouth. Perhaps the camera was new and I was trying it out. Maybe I was trying to annoy my mother. I can't remember now.

I also have a photograph of my mother holding me as a baby under a snowball tree in our backyard. My mother's hair is long and thick and light brown, waved in a style that might have been popular in 1972, when I'd have been a year old. She has on a plaid, open-necked shirt and a rust-colored suede jacket, and I am guessing that the month is September. She looks *present* in the picture, smiling slightly at my father, who'd have been behind the camera. I have on a silly pink hat and seem to be gnawing on my knuckles. I inherited my mother's hair and wide mouth but my father's eyes. After Clara was born, my mother cut her hair, and I never again saw her with it long.

I walk out to the barn and find my father sitting with his coffee in the chair by the stove. On the floor are drifts of sawdust, and in the corners, plastic bags of shavings. The air is suffused with fine particles, like a dissipating fog on a summer day. I watch as he puts the mug on a windowsill and bends his head. He does this often when he doesn't know I'm in the room. He folds his hands, his elbows on his thighs, his legs spread wide. His grief has no texture now — no tears, no ache in the throat, no rage. It is simply darkness, I think, a cloak that sometimes makes it hard for him to breathe.

"Dad," I say.

"Yup," he says, raising his head and turning toward me.

"No school today," I say.

"I didn't think there would be. What time is it?"

"About ten."

"You slept late."

"I did."

Through his shop window and just beyond the pines, I can see a sliver of lake — green glass in summer; blue in fall; and in the winter, simply a wedge of white. To the left of the lake is an abandoned ski hill with only three trails. There are remnants of a chairlift and a small shack at the top. It is said that in years gone by, the operator, a jovial fellow named Al, always saluted each skier as he or she slid off the chair.

Beyond the clearing my father has made, the woods grow immediately dense. In the summer they are full of mosquitoes and blackflies, and I always have to spray myself with Off. My father is thinking of screening in the porch, and I figure that maybe in a year or two he'll get around to it.

"You eat breakfast?" he asks.

"Not yet."

"There's English muffins and jelly."

"I like them sometimes with peanut butter," I say.

"Your mother would mix peanut butter with cottage cheese in a bowl," he says. "It used to make me want to gag, but she liked it so much I never told her how disgusting it was."

I hold my breath and look down into my cup. My father almost never speaks about my mother unless to answer a direct question from me.

I clamp my teeth shut. I know that if my eyes well up, it will be the last memory he'll allow himself to share with me for some time.

In my mind I see a small stone dislodged in a wall, one stone shoved forward until it falls. The other stones shift and settle and try to fill in the space, but still there is a hole through which water, in the form of memory, begins to seep.

Seepage.

In September I had the word in a spelling bee. A simple word, though I got it wrong, spelling it *seapage,* which, if you think about it, is not entirely illogical.

"I bet we could find the spot," I say, announcing the reason I've come to find him. "When we get close enough, the orange tapes will give the place away."

I have again an image of the baby still in the sleeping bag. What if we didn't take that walk yesterday? I am thinking. What if we didn't find her? Good luck, I'm beginning to discover, is just as baffling as the bad. There never seems to be a reason for it — no sense of reward or punishment. It simply *is* — the most incomprehensible idea of all.

I wonder if there are still police guarding the site. I decide there won't be: what reason would they have had to stay? The crime is over, all evidence surely collected. I imagine the sleeping bag and the bloody towel safely tucked away inside plastic bags on a shelf at a police station. I think of the detective with his scars. The detective, who will be busy now with a different crime.

My father is silent.

"Okay then," I say. "I'll just go myself."

In the back hallway, I take my jacket off the hook and put on my hat and mittens. Just outside the back door, I lace up my showshoes and take a step forward. The shoes have no traction on the ice. I lurch, flailing for something to hold on to. After a dozen steps and one hard fall, I slide backwards to the house, hugging the wall, trying to keep the shoes from skidding out from under me. I undo the straps. If my father has seen me slipping and sliding and has had a chuckle over it, he never says so.

I go back inside the house. I make myself an English muffin with peanut butter and think about my mother with her cottage cheese. I walk upstairs to my room, which is decorated with a Yankees pennant and a poster of Garfield. On one wall I've been painting a multi-colored mural of all the ski hills in New England — Sunday River, Attitash, Loon Mountain, Bromley, Killington, King Ridge, Sunapee, and others. It took me all of Christmas vacation the year before to sketch the outline, and I think it's quite a good map in geographical relief. All the mountains I have skied are capped with snow; the hills I have yet to ski remain green. Also in my room is the only radio allowed in the house. The deal my father and I have made is that I can listen to whatever I want, as long as it can't be heard outside my room. Sometimes my father will ask me to go upstairs and get the weather report, but that's all he ever wants to know from the radio.

We don't have a television, and we don't get the newspaper. When we first moved to New Hampshire, my father tried the local newspaper. One morning there was a front-page story about a woman who had backed over her fourteen-month-old son with her Olds Cutlass. My father rose from the den, walked into the kitchen, stuffed the paper into the trash can, and that was that.

I have an easel and paints in my room and a chair that can be made into a single bed on the rare occasion I have a friend come to visit. I make beaded jewelry on my desk and read on my bed. My father used to ask me to make my bed until I pointed out that he never made his, and so he stopped speaking to me about it. I hate going to the Laundromat and wish we had a washing machine. I have asked for one for Christmas.

In the afternoon, while I'm reading, I hear a dripping

that sounds like a summer rain. I go to the window and look out. The ice has begun to thaw. The world around the house is softening, the crust relenting.

I walk out to the barn.

"All right," my father says, looking up. "Let's go."

Walking on snowshoes in heavy melting snow, however, is nearly as difficult as walking on ice. Each footfall digs into the melted crust, shoving us off balance. My legs begin to ache before we've gone a hundred feet. The light turns flat, the worst sort of light for walking or skiing. I can't see the bumps or the ruts, and sometimes it feels as though we're coasting on fog. We cross the expanse of what in the summer would be lawn and then enter the trees.

I squint into the ugly light, trying to follow the thin imprints on the snow of yesterday's trek. Occasionally we have to guess at the precise route because a layer of blown snow covered the tracks before the freeze. I see the trail in reverse, and I remember our frantic run of the day before with the baby in my father's arms. My breath comes hard and fast, and I see that my father has increased his pace as well. We search for the place where we stopped climbing and veered sideways around the hill, lured on by the baby's cries. I can't shake the notion that she was calling out specifically to us.

Come get me.

Above us a thin wind begins to whine through the pines, bending the tips and sending small clumps of snow to the ground, dotting the surface of the crust with baseballs. I am wet with sweat inside my parka. I unzip it and let the frigid air cool my skin. I take off my hat and stuff it into a pocket. I brush away the low boughs with my hands. I think that we have lost the tracks, but my father just keeps pushing forward.

My father owns twenty acres of rock, hardwood, and sloped fields. All the wood for his furniture comes from his acreage: walnut and oak and maple; pine and cherry and tamarack. The local lumberyard sawed and planed the lumber, laying in a supply of smooth planks that my father won't use up for years.

After a time, my father finds our earlier tracks, and we follow them at a slower pace. When we've gone for about fifteen minutes, I see, in the distance, a sliver of orange tape. "There it is," I say.

We make our way to the place that has been cordoned off. A circle of tape has been threaded through the trees. It funnels off into a path back to the motel, as if for a bride returning from an outdoor wedding. Within the circle is the soft place where the sleeping bag was, a print of my father's snowshoe outlined in a thin stream of red spray paint, and, similarly outlined, a size ten and a half bootprint. Neither of us noticed the bootprint the night before. I wonder if the police found my father's flashlight, if it's worth trying to get it back. Did my father tell Detective Warren about the flashlight? I try to remember. Will they think it was the other guy's and waste a lot of time trying to track it down?

We walk around the circle and stand with our backs to the motel. I examine the soft place where the sleeping bag was.

"Dad," I say. "Why did he put the baby in a sleeping bag if he meant to kill her?"

My father looks up at the bare tree limbs. "I don't know," he says. "I guess he didn't want her to be cold."

"That doesn't make any sense," I say.

"None of it makes any sense."

I pull on the plastic tape, seeing if it will stretch. "What do you think they'll call her?" I ask.

"I don't know," he says.

"Maybe they'll give her our last name," I say. "Maybe she'll be called Baby Dillon. Remember how they called Clara 'Baby Baker-Dillon'?"

We stand for a time in silence, and I know that my father is thinking about Baby Baker-Dillon. I can feel it coming off him in waves. I have the tape looped around my mitten now.

"Dad," I say.

"What?"

"Why was there so much blood and stuff in the motel room?"

My father picks up some soft wet snow and starts to fashion it into a ball. "There's some blood when a woman gives birth," he says. "And there's something called the placenta, which is full of blood and which is the thing that nourishes the baby. It comes out after the birth."

"I know about that," I say.

"So all of that blood was natural. It doesn't mean that the woman was hurt or injured."

"But it *does* hurt, right?"

In the flat light my father looks old. The skin beneath his lower lids is almost lavender in color and loose with wrinkles. "It hurts," he says carefully, "but every birth is different."

"Did Mom hurt when I was born?"

My father whacks the ball against the tree. "Yes, she did," he says. "And if she were here, she would tell you that every minute was worth it."

A crunch of snow startles both of us. We turn to see Detective Warren, with his crimson-muffled neck, not twenty feet away. "Didn't mean to startle you," he says.

"Like hell," my father says under his breath.

Warren stands with his hands in his overcoat pockets, a man out for an unlikely stroll behind a motel in the dead of winter. "Went to your place, no one answered the door.

Drove over here on a hunch." He moves a step closer. "You had to see the spot again, didn't you?"

He is walking in the prints made by the technicians the night before, placing each Timberland boot into a hole.

"People are predictable, Mr. Dillon," he says. "We go back to the places that once gave us a jolt. Lovers do it all the time."

He keeps moving toward us, one careful footfall at a time. "You're all over the papers today, Mr. Dillon. I'm surprised I didn't see Channel 5 at your place. Your house is wide open, by the way."

"You went inside," my father says.

"I was looking for you to tell you about the girl. I drove all the way up your road, and I wasn't going to leave without seeing if you were in. You make nice stuff, by the way."

My father is silent, refusing to be drawn in by the compliment.

"The baby's doing fine," Warren says.

My father bangs a snowshoe against a mound of hard-packed snow.

"We're on the same side here, Mr. Dillon," Warren says.

"What side would that be?"

"You found the baby and saved her life," Warren says, shooting a cigarette from a pack of Camels. He lights it with a lighter. "You smoke?" he asks.

My father shakes his head, even though he does.

"Then I find the guy who did it," Warren says. "That's how it works. We're a team."

"We're not a team," my father says.

"I called down to Westchester," Warren says, "and spoke to a guy named Thibodeau. You remember Thibodeau?"

Even I remember Thibodeau. Officer Thibodeau came to our house the morning after the accident with the news we already knew. My father shouted at him to get off our goddamn steps.

"A terrible thing," Warren says. "I probably would have done the same as you — moved away, reinvented my life. Don't know where I'd have gone, though. Maybe Canada, maybe the city. Anonymity in the city."

I have the orange tape wrapped around my mittens. I give it another tug.

"I got two boys, eight and ten," Warren says.

"Let's go, Nicky," my father says.

"I want this guy," Warren says.

"I think we're done here," my father says.

The detective drops the barely smoked butt onto the snow. He pulls his gloves out of his pocket and puts them on.

"No one's done here," Warren says.

When we return to the house, my father calls Dr. Gibson. I hang around in the den so that I can hear him in the kitchen.

"I just wondered how the baby was doing," I hear my father say into the phone.

"That's good, right?" my father says.

"Where is she now?" he asks.

"She'll be there how long? . . .

"Does she have a name yet? . . .

"Baby Doris," my father repeats. He sounds surprised, taken aback. "You say she'll go into foster care? . . .

"It seems so —"

Dr. Gibson must make a comment about foster care and adoption, because my father says, "Yes, cold."

I can hear my father pouring himself a cup of coffee. "When the system doesn't work, what happens? . . .

"She'd be prosecuted, though. . . ."

"Thanks," my father says. "I just wanted to know that the baby was okay."

My father hangs up the phone. I move into the kitchen. He's sipping the lukewarm coffee and looking out the kitchen window. "Hey," he says when he hears me.

"She's all right?" I ask.

"She's fine."

"They've named her Baby Doris?"

"Apparently." He sets the mug down. "Going to Sweetser's," he says. "Want to come?"

I don't have to be asked twice to accompany my father on a trip to town.

My father holds the door for me when we enter the hardware store. Mr. Sweetser looks up from the paper he has spread across the counter next to the register. "Our local hero," he says.

"You heard," my father says.

"Front page. See for yourself."

My father and I make our way to the counter. In a newspaper known for its high-school sports news, Sunday comics, and coupons, I can see a headline that reads INFANT FOUND IN SNOW. Below that is another, smaller headline: *Local Carpenter Finds Baby Alive in Bloody Sleeping Bag*. I bend closer to the counter and read the paper with my father. The reporter has largely got the story right. There is mention of the motel, the Volvo, and the navy peacoat. There is no mention of me.

"Got your name spelled wrong," Sweetser says.

"Yeah, I saw that," my father says.

Dylan. It happens all the time.

"You want me to cut it out for you?"

My father shakes his head.

"So what happened?" Sweetser asks.

My father unzips his jacket. The store is heated by a fickle woodstove in the corner that makes the temperature fluctuate between ninety degrees and sixty. Today it feels like eighty. "Nicky and I were taking a walk when we heard a cry," my father says. "We thought it might be an animal at first. And then we heard the sound of a car door shutting."

"The baby was in a sleeping bag?" Sweetser asks.

My father nods.

"Weirdest thing," Sweetser says, smoothing the pink strands of hair over his head. He has recently shaved his beard, revealing a sunken chin and strange pale skin like a new layer on an animal that's just molted. "You wouldn't think."

"No, you wouldn't think," my father says.

"It's like those fairy tales my wife used to read the kids," Sweetser says. "Carpenter goes into the woods and finds a baby."

"In a fairy tale it would be a princess," my father says.

"You should be so lucky," Sweetser says.

For a hardware store in the no-man's-land between Hanover and Concord, Sweetser's carries an impressive array of tools. Sweetser likes their heft and shape, he says, much as my father does. Beyond the shelves of tools are other shelves, of Pyrex dishes, boxes of Miracle-Gro (dusty now in the off-season), and cans of Sherwin-Williams paint. Attached to the store is a smaller, shedlike annex in which Sweetser sells antiques, the word *antiques* used loosely. Much of the furniture is from the sixties.

"That couple make it up to your place last Friday?" Sweetser asks.

"What couple?"

"I sent some tourists your way when they started asking for a Shaker table. I said you did stuff that looked like Shaker."

"Never saw them," my father says.

"Your road is crap," Sweetser says.

Sweetser has been saying our road is crap ever since we moved into town. For over a year now, he's been sending people my father's way. Only a half dozen so far have braved the miserable road, but by the time they make the trek, they almost always buy something.

"I need a level," my father says.

"What happened to the old one?"

"I cracked the vial."

"Hard to do."

"Yeah. Well."

My father moves to the shelf of levels. His old level, which worked perfectly well until he knocked the glass vial against the refrigerator, had metal rails. He picks up a wooden level. Some of the vials, I see, are oval, while others are arched. My father points out to me a level that reads in a 360-degree direction.

"Going to Remy's for a coffee," Sweetser says, sliding his arm into a yellow plaid jacket. "You want one?"

"No thanks," my father says.

"A Drake's?"

"No, that's okay. I had breakfast."

"Nicky, how about you?" Sweetser asks. "You want one?"

"A Drake's coffee cake?" I ask.

"She wants one," Sweetser says.

When Sweetser has left the store, I tell my father I need white paint. "I'm skiing Gunstock with Jo after Christmas."

"How many now?" he asks.

"Seven," I say, referring to the white peaks of my mural.

"When are you going?" my father asks.

"The day after Christmas."

"Have you said yes definitely?"

"What's wrong? Can't I go?"

"Grammie will still be here," my father says.

"So I can't go skiing?" I ask, my tone immediately challenging. I can go from zero to all-out rage in less than five seconds now.

"No, you can go," my father says. "You should ask first is what I'm saying. I might have had plans. We might have been going somewhere."

"Dad," I say, my voice notched up to incredulity, "we never go *anywhere*."

I pick out a pint of linen white and walk over to study the antiques. There's a maple bedroom set and a ratty green plaid sofa. A jukebox is in a corner. I wonder if it works.

Sweetser puts his shoulder to the door and enters bearing a coffee cup and a Drake's cake. My father selects the level with the fixed vial. He brings it to the counter and pays for it. With my father's change, Sweetser gives him a small rectangle of newsprint.

"Cut it out anyway," Sweetser says.

My father pulls out of Sweetser's parking lot, the level and the clipping on my lap. He heads in the direction of home. I take a bite of the Drake's cake, the crumbs falling down the front of my parka. "Dad," I say. "We need food."

"You make a list?"

"No, but we need milk and Cheerios," I say. "Bread for sandwiches. Bologna. Stuff for dinner."

"I don't want to go to Remy's," he says. "Enough of the local hero stuff."

My father does a 180 and heads for Butson's Market, a store further out of town that he can sometimes get in and out of without running into anyone he knows. We pass the Mobil station and the Shepherd Village School, a one-room schoolhouse built in 1780. The school houses the town's K–6; the playground is a gravel front yard. Older students are bused out of town to the Regional, a trip that takes, in my case, forty minutes each way.

Beside the school is the Congregational Church, a white clapboarded building with long windows and black shutters. The church has a steeply pitched roof and a tower with a bell. Neither my father nor I has ever been inside it.

We pass the three stately homes in town, one after another on a hill, two of which have seen better days. We pass Serenity Carpets, a beige house trailer, the volunteer fire department (Bingo Every Thursday Nite 6:30), and Croydon Realty, to which we drifted in a slow stop the first time we came into town — Croydon Realty, where it's still possible to buy a house for $26,000; not much of a house, but a house. In the summers my father and I sometimes go for exploratory drives around the countryside, getting lost on backwoods roads, finding small pockets of surprisingly well tended houses. "How do they make a living?" my father will always ask. Once we came upon a moose ambling along in front of us, hogging the narrow road. We had to follow it for twenty minutes at five miles an hour, not daring to pass it, learning to like the gentle jog of the animal's rump.

After Croydon Realty, there are four miles of nothing — just woods with a stream that parallels the road. My father slows as he passes Mercy, the first set of buildings after the gap, the hospital housed in what was once a brick, four-story hotel, converted in the 1930s. Though it has since sprouted modern wings, the words *De Wolfe Hotel 1898* are still inscribed over the front door of the original building.

"Dad, let's stop," I say. "I want to see her."

My father stares at the hospital. I know that he would like to see the baby, too. But after a few seconds, he shakes his head. "Too much red tape," he says, accelerating.

Beyond the hospital is a strip mall into which my father turns. He stops in front of a sign that reads *Liquor Outlet, Butson's Market, Family Dollar, Frank Renata D.D.S.*

Milk, I think. Cheerios. Coffee. Chicken with Stars. American cheese. Hamburger meat. Maybe some Ring Dings.

With a week's worth of groceries, my father makes the reverse trip — past the hospital, through the gap, then the

Realtor, the three stately homes, and Remy's and Sweet-ser's right across the street from each other. Our own road is six miles out of town. Along the way we pass houses with front porches filled with couches and plastic toys and empty propane tanks. One of these houses is a small white clapboard cottage with a tiny fenced-in backyard. The front porch is neatly crowded with bicycles and tricycles, baseball bats and hockey sticks. Evidence of boys can also be found in the wash on the line: T-shirts in varying sizes, jeans, and hockey shirts or bathing suits depending on the season. In the middle of the wash I sometimes see a bra or a slip or a pretty nightgown. When we drive by in the win-ter, we occasionally see the mother struggling with large, unwieldy frozen sheets. They look like cardboard and blow with the wind. I always wave at the woman, who smiles and waves back. Sometimes in the summers I have an urge to stop my bike and say hello and enter that house and meet the boys and see the chaos I imagine there.

My father pulls the truck into our driveway. "You bought spaghetti?" he asks.

"And Ragú sauce," I say.

He parks in his usual spot beside the barn. He turns off the engine. "That okay for supper?"

"It's fine."

"I bought Breyers," he says.

"I saw."

"Butter pecan. Your favorite."

"Dad?" I say.

"What?"

"How did the baby get named Doris?"

My father reaches for his cigarettes, a nervous gesture, but then he decides against it with me in the truck. "I don't know," he says. "Maybe it was the name of one of the nurses."

"It sounds like the name of a hurricane."

"They probably have a system," he says.

"You think they get that many babies?"

"I don't think so. I hope not."

"It's an old-fashioned name," I say. I am leaning against my door. My father has his hand on his door handle, as if he were anxious to get out of the truck.

"It's a strange name to give a baby these days," he concedes.

"What will happen to her?" I ask. "Did Dr. Gibson tell you?"

"She'll go into social services," my father says. He puts his hand on the door handle and opens the door a crack.

"She'll get a new mother and father and new brothers and sisters?"

"Most likely."

"It doesn't seem right," I say.

"What doesn't seem right?"

"Us not knowing where she is."

"That's the way it has to be, Nicky." He opens his door, signaling the end of the conversation.

"Dad?" I ask.

"What?"

"Why can't we have her? We could go get her and have her with us."

The idea is both appalling and sublime. In my twelve-year-old mind, I have conceived the notion of supplanting one baby with another. As soon as I say the words and catch a glimpse of my father's face, I see what I've done. But as a twelve-year-old will do, I become defensive. "Why not?" I ask with the petulant tone of the aggrieved and misunderstood, a tone I will shortly learn to master. "Didn't it make you feel like maybe Clara had come back to us? That maybe we're supposed to have her?"

My father steps out of the truck. He takes a long breath. "No, Nicky, it did not," he says. "Clara was Clara, and this baby is someone else. She is not ours to have." He looks over at the barn and then back at me. "Help me get these groceries in the house before the ice cream melts."

"Dad, it's *twenty* out," I say. "The ice cream isn't going anywhere."

But I am saying this to my father's back. He has shut the door and taken a bag of groceries from the back of the truck. I watch him walk toward the house, grief a hard nut inside his chest.

That night the snow freezes again, and a ferocious wind blows. I wake to the sound of limbs snapping under the weight of the ice. The cracks resound like gunshots — some muffled, some as sharp as fireworks. The noise rouses me from my bed at daybreak, and I wait at my bedroom window for the light to come up. The woods beyond the cleared lot is littered with broken trees, their branches bent to the ground, as though a hurricane had come and gone.

I hear my father on the stairs. I put on my bathrobe and slippers and find him in the kitchen standing beside the Mr. Coffee, waiting for the machine to fill the pot. He's leaning against the sink in his stocking feet, his arms crossed against yet another flannel shirt. His jeans are the same ones he's been wearing for a week, and I note that his beard can no longer be called stubble.

"Dad," I say, "maybe you should shave."

"I'm thinking of growing a beard." He rubs his chin.

"Maybe you should shave."

A trickle of coffee emerges from the coffeemaker.

"Trees keep you up?" he asks.

"They woke me up."

"Lot of clearing in the spring." He bends slightly to look out the window. "I'm worried about the roof with all this heavy snow and ice. The pitch is too shallow in the front. I should have done the roof in the fall. I hate roofing."

"Why?"

"I get vertigo."

"What's vertigo?" I ask.

"Fear of heights. I get dizzy."

This is a fact I haven't known about my father. I wonder what else I don't know. He pours himself a cup of coffee. I open the fridge and take out the milk.

"I should get up there and shovel," he says.

"I'll help you," I say with enthusiasm. The idea of being able to climb onto the roof and survey our little kingdom is an exciting one.

"I hate roofing," he says, "but on the other hand, I don't relish the idea of a crew hanging out here for the duration of the job."

This goes without saying.

"Another week," he says, "and then you're out for Christmas vacation."

At Christmas, my grandmother will come, as she always does, and cook for us and put up stockings and "make a good Christmas," as she likes to say. My father will go through the motions, but I like the cookies and the cloved oranges and the sight of presents scattered around a tree.

"You'd better get dressed," he says, "or you'll miss the bus."

"You think we should check first? That maybe it's another snow day?"

"I think you should get dressed," he says.

At school, I am famous. Though the papers haven't mentioned my name, everyone seems to know that I was there when the baby was found. I am asked for details, easy to deliver. I tell about hearing the cries and finding the infant and going to the hospital and being questioned by a detective.

"The sleeping bag was bloody?" Jo asks me at my locker. Jo is nearly as tall as my father. She has blond hair that streams back from her face, like the goddess at the prow of a Viking ship.

"A little," I say. "It was mostly the towel that was bloody."

"So when you give birth, there's blood?" she asks.

"Of course," I say.

"Where does the blood come from?"

"The placenta," I say, banging my locker shut.

"Oh," Jo says, puzzled.

The fact that I'd come from New York was regarded as exotic when I first arrived in New Hampshire. And it was certainly in my favor that I wasn't a Masshole, which is how some of the locals refer to the people who live one state south. Still, I've worked it out that it will take at least two generations, maybe three, before the natives stop referring to my father and me as newcomers.

I have two friends at school — the Viking goddess and Roger Kelly. The three of us eat lunch together and share some classes, and Roger and I are in the school band. Making arrangements to see Jo or Roger after school or on weekends is difficult, however: everything has to be thought about in advance. Jo's mother has made no secret of the fact that she hates the long drive up to our house, and I think she regards my father as suspicious. If there's to be a sleepover, I usually stay at Jo's. I don't have sleepovers with Roger, of course, but we sometimes play basketball after school, and I come home on the late bus.

When I lived in New York, I had more than two friends. There were four fourth-grade classes in my elementary school alone, and there were three elementary schools in our town. I went to sleepovers often and had them at my house as well. I took dance lessons and gymnastics and was a Brownie and a Girl Scout. I had a lavender-and-white bedroom with a canopy bed, and I could fit six or seven girls and their sleeping bags on the thick carpet. We watched movies in the living room and then went upstairs at eleven, which is the latest my parents would let us stay up. We did our nails or played Truth or Dare until after midnight, learning how to fall down giggling without waking my parents.

When Clara was six months old, she was moved into her own bedroom next to mine. My friends liked to play with her when they came to visit. They tried to braid her hair, but she never had enough hair for any braid to be satisfying. Her room was yellow and orange and blue, largely because I'd painted one wall with yellow and orange and blue fish, in different shapes and sizes, fish such as you'd never come across in a lifetime, even in the Caribbean. I sometimes used to wonder, after we moved to New Hampshire, what the new owners did with that room, if they left the yellow and orange and blue fish swimming through the water, or if they painted the wall white, erasing my artwork the way our family seemed to have been erased — with one large roller.

When I first moved to Shepherd, I was ragged and raw and prone to sudden fits of weeping, difficult to hide in a one-room schoolhouse. To compensate for my lack of emotional control, I pretended to an air of weariness and disdain, as if as a New Yorker I was so far ahead of my peers that I hardly need bother to pay attention in class. I was disabused of this notion in a gradual way, and by May I'd finally caught up in math.

In the scrub on our land were dozens of raspberry bushes that my father and I stumbled across one July day the first summer in New Hampshire. We picked the berries and brought them back to the house and, for a time, ate them with everything (on cereal, on ice cream, with steak). Because there were more raspberries on the land than he and I could consume, I decided to sell them at the end of the road. My father encouraged me to ask Sweetser if he knew where I might come by a few dozen wooden fruit boxes. Sweetser, who seemed to be able to procure almost anything on demand, sold me several tall stacks for five dollars, waiving the payment and calling it a loan, which I repaid with pride at the end of the first week.

Each morning, in my denim shorts and pastel T-shirts, I would pick the raspberries in the brush and put them in a basket that hung from my shoulder. When I had enough berries, I'd ride my bicycle the length of our dirt road to its entrance. There I had a card table and a plastic lawn chair set up. I'd fill the fruit boxes with the raspberries and then sit and wait. I could count on at least four customers a day: a woman whose name I never did learn, but who seemed to have a lot of houseguests; Mrs. Clapper, who was a visiting nurse and who used to take a box each day to one of her patients; Mr. Bolduc, who went by every morning to get the newspaper and his mail in town; and Mr. Sweetser, who had no reason that I could ever see to drive by our road, but there he was (I don't believe he ever missed a day). I might have four or five other customers who were doubtless so surprised to see a girl selling raspberries on that remote wooded road that they felt a moral obligation to stop. Altogether I would spend an hour picking the berries, twenty minutes riding to and fro on my bike, and three or four hours at the stand — an approximate total of six hours. I sold the berries for seventy-five cents a box, and if lucky I'd make six dollars a day. Six days at the stand (some days spent under a rigged umbrella when it rained) might yield thirty-six dollars a week, which, when I was ten and eleven years old, seemed a small fortune. I would sit in my chair and sometimes read, but mostly I'd stare off into space, occasionally noticing the way a pair of monarchs folded into each other when they mated, or the way the Queen Anne's lace seemed to have popped open overnight. I learned to daydream that summer, and it was then that I conceived of the idea of Clara as still growing. She'd have been almost two years old that first summer and probably a nuisance, but I imagined her wandering into weeds and wildflowers, the top of her head lost below the yellow and magenta blossoms, or reaching for a raspberry and tipping over a pint box. I imagined her on her tummy on top of my card table taking a nap while I stroked her back.

Sunday is the anniversary of my mother's and Clara's deaths. I know it and my father knows it, but neither of us speaks of it all day. I know my father remembers, because he keeps walking from the barn to the house and back to the barn again, as if he can't decide what to do with himself. He looks at me when he thinks I'm not aware of it. He wants to say something but is unsure of what will happen to both of us if he does. He takes a shower at midday, which he almost never does, and spends a long time in his bedroom, where I know there is a picture of my mother and me and Clara. I am twelve and keenly aware of milestones and anniversaries, and I think the day should be marked.

"Dad," I say when he finally comes out of the bedroom. "Can we go to Butson's Market?"

"What for?" he asks.

"I think they sell flowers there."

He doesn't ask me what the flowers are for.

The sun has been out for two days. I wear my jacket open. My father has on only a sweater. He's shaved, and his hair is clean, and he's not an embarrassment to be with, which is an improvement over the previous year. On the first anniversary of the accident, my father sat in the barn all day and didn't move. I felt lonely and sad and in need of comfort, but I didn't have the courage to walk to the barn and see what I might find there: my father in the Dad position, his mouth open as if his nose were stuffed, his eyes vacant, seeing only images from the past. Instead I looked through my album, made a beaded necklace, answered the phone when my grandmother called, and then I cried for so long that she finally insisted I go get my father.

At Butson's Market, my father searches for dishwashing liquid while I stand in front of the refrigerated shelves that hold the bunches of flowers. There are daisies and carnations, baby's breath and roses, and even though the bouquets are all more or less alike, I spend a lot of time trying to decide which is best. The carnations look fake pink and bother me. One bouquet, almost entirely yellow, has a long creepy-looking flower in its center that might be a lily.

"That one's pretty," my father says, pointing to a bouquet that is mostly lavender and white.

"What are those bluish-purple flowers?" I ask.

"I don't know."

"Do you think Mom would like them?"

"I think she would," he says.

I clutch the bouquet all the way home, trying to decide where to put it. We have a Mason jar in a cabinet in the kitchen. I'll arrange them in that, I think, but I won't leave them in the kitchen. I could set them on the coffee table in the den, though that seems a little ordinary to me. If I put them in my father's room, I won't be able to see them. In the end, I set them on the shelf in the back hallway. I sit across from the flowers on the bench and admire them. My father says, "They look nice," as he goes out to the barn.

But something is still bothering me. They don't seem right inside the house, and more important, I'm afraid my mother and Clara won't be able to see them. It's illogical, of course — if Clara and my mother have become spirits who actually *can* see down to Earth, then surely they can see through houses — but I can't shake the notion. I put on my jacket and walk the Mason jar to the edge of the clearing before the woods begin. I set the jar in the snow.

I stand back. The flowers seem more alive in the sunshine. I know they'll die before morning, but I am oddly satisfied.

I think about my mother and Clara. I shut my eyes. I imagine them vividly. I do this periodically in order to keep the images clear and sharp. The pictures in my mind have warmth and smell and movement, treasures I cannot afford to lose.

On the last day before Christmas vacation, we have a party in our homeroom at school. In New York we had combined Hanukkah-Christmas celebrations, but in New Hampshire it is simply a Christmas party, there being no one in our school in need of Hanukkah. Gifts are exchanged, and the boys are annoyingly manic because of the half day. I've drawn Molly Curran's name and have given her, in keeping with a lifelong propensity to give gifts I really want for myself, a kit with twenty different colors of nail polish in it. I've gotten a tape of the Police from Billy Brock, who's clearly operating on the same principle and, worse, doesn't know me very well, since I don't own a tape player. On the bus on the way home from school, I debate asking my father for a tape player instead of a washing machine for Christmas. Is it too late, I wonder, to ask for both?

After I hang up my jacket, I find my father in his shop. He's consumed with preparations for a glue-up, a precise and panicky procedure that in fifteen minutes can ruin weeks of painstaking woodwork. One has to set the glue, bring the components together, apply suitable clamping pressure, test the squareness, and then clean up the excess — all in about a minute and a half. My father is making a drawer, the first of two that will be fitted into the openings of a small sideboard he has to finish before Christmas. It is his first commission.

"How was school?" he asks.

"Good," I say.

"Last day."

"Yup."

"How was the party?"

"Good."

"What did you get?"

"A tape of the Police."

I look him in the eye and hope he is thinking, *Tape player: good idea for Nicky for Christmas.*

The day marks a week and two days since my father and I walked into the woods and found a baby. I've been unable to keep from thinking about what might have happened to Baby Doris had we not found her. I've imagined the sleeping bag a frozen cocoon with long icicles falling like daggers all around her. In a second call to Dr. Gibson, my father learned that the baby's toes would not have to be amputated. "She's a fighter," the doctor told my father, a comment which, when relayed to me, filled me with pride. We also learned that she is to be collected today by social services and delivered to a temporary foster home. This information upset me greatly when I heard it, since I liked having the baby in the hospital, having her contained there. We won't be told where she is going. The whole process strikes me as being a lot like the witness protection program, with its anonymity and its new cast of characters: new mother, new father, new brothers and sisters. We won't even be told the baby's new name. Forever, to us, she will have to be Baby Doris.

I leave my father and walk back into the house and into

the kitchen, where I make myself a cup of hot chocolate. I stick an English muffin into the toaster and have an image of my mother mixing up a bowl of cottage cheese and peanut butter. Just the day before, I had a memory of my mother in her garden, bent straight over, her legs tanned, her shorts riding high on her thighs. My father was on the John Deere, headed toward my swing set. Because he was staring at my mother (trying, I think now, to get a good look at her from the front), he mowed right into the swing set, the prow of the John Deere catching on a swing and riding it up into the air. My father leapt off backwards and rolled out of the way. The engine cut out as he fell, but when he stood the mower was still stuck in the swing, its nose pointed skyward. My mother began to laugh, putting the back of her hand to her mouth.

And last night I had a memory of my mother lying beside my father on their bed, the loose strap of the slip in which she slept revealing part of an engorged breast. They were talking softly so as not to wake Clara, barely a week old, in a cot next to the bed. What had they been talking about? Why had I gone into the room? I can't remember. As they whispered, a stain began to blossom on my mother's slip, the milk leaking with surprising fluidity, an enormous flowering. I remember my mother's hand going to her breast and her whispering to my father, *Oh, Rob; oh, look.*

In the kitchen I smell smoke. The English muffin is

stuck in the toaster. I pull the plug, remove the muffin with a fork, and Frisbee the charred puck into the sink.

I hear a knock then, and I think it's a branch tapping against the side of the house. Then I hear the human rhythm: three taps, a pause. Another three. Another pause. I think it might be the detective again, and I wonder if I should say my father isn't home. But what if the detective just barges through and finds out I am lying? Can I be prosecuted for lying to an officer of the law? I move to the cloakroom and open the door.

A couple stands on the steps, and I see behind them that it has begun snowing lightly. The woman has large, square glasses with blue-tinted frames and a hairdo one can't come by in the entire state of New Hampshire: sleek and thick and blunt cut. She wears glossy lipstick the color of cherries that matches her leather gloves. She has on a white down jacket she clearly hasn't bought at L. L. Bean. The man unzips his black ski parka, smiles, and says, "We heard down at the antiques store that someone called Mr. Dillon makes furniture that looks like Shaker. Are we in the right place?"

I say, yes, they are, but I am puzzled. Hasn't it been more than a week since Sweetser told the couple about my father's furniture? Where have they been in the meantime? In a time warp? I tell them to come inside because of the snow and that I'll be right back. I have to get my father, I add.

"Dad," I say when I reach his shop, "there are two people here who want to see your furniture."

I've interrupted him in the middle of the glue-up. He shakes his head vigorously, as if to say, *For heaven's sake, Nicky, not now.*

"I'll take them to the front room," I offer.

The man and the woman stomp the snow from their boots onto the mat. I tell them that my dad will be with them soon, and that I'll take them to see the furniture. The woman glances over at the man and smiles, as if to say, *Isn't she cute?*

We walk through the kitchen and the dining room that is now a den. We pass the room my father and I never enter, the room that is like a shrine. I show them into the front room, where the furniture is: two straight-back chairs; three small tables; a low, square cocktail table; a walnut dining table; an oak bookcase; and a small cabinet.

"My goodness," the woman says.

"I see what the man at the antiques store meant," the man says. "This looks very much like Shaker."

"Simple but beautiful," the woman says.

"Good finish," the man says.

I wonder if they are complimenting my father's work for my benefit; if when I leave the room, negative comments will emerge. When people come to look at the furniture, my father almost always excuses himself and goes outside for a smoke. He hates being a salesman. Customers usually come in pairs — couples from Massachusetts or New York looking to take something back with them to the house or the apartment, something to remember the weekend or the vacation by. I am idly thinking about how to bug the showroom when my father enters, wiping his hands on a rag. "Sorry about that," he says as he crosses the threshold.

My father hasn't shaved, and he hasn't cut his hair. The lids of his eyes are pink-rimmed. Oh God, has he been crying? No, I tell myself, it's the glue; his eyes are pink because of the fumes. He's covered with sawdust, and he looks, frankly, frightening.

There's a moment of silence. Two moments anyway. Enough to make me look over at the man, who is staring at my father, and then over at my father, who is staring back at him.

"Robert?" the man asks.

"Steve," my father says.

The two men advance to shake each other's hand.

"I heard you'd moved somewhere in New England," Steve says in a disbelieving voice, as if he cannot credit what he is seeing. "I just never thought . . . Virginia, this is Robert Dillon. We used to work together in the city."

Virginia steps forward and shakes my father's hand. His hand is rough and callused, and I know it smells of turpentine.

"This is my daughter, Nicky," my father says.

"We've met," Steve says, smiling in my direction. "She showed us in."

There's another moment of silence.

"Well," Steve says. "Your work is beautiful. Just beautiful. Isn't it, Virginia?"

"Yes," Virginia says. "Very beautiful. The man at the antiques store was right. It bears a strong resemblance to Shaker."

I glance at my father, and his face makes my stomach feel hollow.

"Listen," Steve says, putting his hand to his forehead. "I just wanted to say . . . I never got a chance to tell you how sorry I was. About . . . you know."

My father gives a quick shake of his head.

"You remember," Steve says to his girlfriend or his wife. "I told you about the man whose wife and baby . . . ?"

"Oh! Oh, yes!" Virginia says in a gush of comprehension. "Oh, I'm so sorry," she adds. "It must have been so hard."

My father is silent. Virginia clutches her pocketbook to her chest. Steve clears his throat and looks around the room.

"Are you still with Porter?" my father asks.

"No, I'm on my own now," Steve says with apparent relief at the change of subject. "I bought two condos in a building on Fifty-seventh Street a year ago." He pauses. "Worth twice what I paid for them already. We live in one,

and I use the other for an office. I've got three guys working for me."

"Phillip still at the old place?" my father asks.

"Phillip," Steve says, shaking his head, as if he can't just
now remember who Phillip is. "Oh, Phillip," he says. "No,
Phillip's moved on. To San Francisco."

"Well," my father says.

"Well," Steve says.

The silence that follows is a white noise inside my head.

"Are you up here for a vacation?" my father asks after a
time.

"Yes," Steve says, once again looking relieved. "We're
skiing different mountains. We went up to Loon and to
Sunday River. Over to Killington. Where else did we go,
Virginia? We're headed home on Friday. Taking advantage
of the early snow this year, you know, before the Christmas crowds." Next to my father, Steve looks polished to a
high sheen. "How about you? You do any skiing?"

"Used to," my father says.

"I do," I say simultaneously.

"We mostly snowshoe now," my father says. "In the
woods."

Steve glances toward the window, as if searching for the
woods. "Snowshoeing," he says, considering. "Like to try
that sometime."

"Yes," Virginia says. "I've always wanted to try that."

"Must be quite a workout," Steve says.

"It can be," my father says.

"So," Steve says, glancing around the room again. "We've been looking for a cocktail table. And I think, Virginia, we just might have found what we're looking for." He moves to my father's table and runs his hand along the finish. I'm wondering if Steve and Virginia would be at all interested in the table if it weren't my father's, if my father hadn't lost his wife and baby, if my father didn't look as though he was on his last dime.

"What kind of wood is this?" Steve asks.

"Cherry," my father says.

"So it's this color naturally," Steve says. "Not a stain."

"No, it's natural. It'll darken up over time."

"Really. What kind of finish is this?"

"Wax over polyurethane," my father says.

"What grade are you in?" Virginia asks, taking a Chap-Stick out of her pocketbook and running it across her lips.

"I'm in seventh grade," I say.

She smacks her lips together. "So you're . . ."

"Twelve."

"That's a good age," she says, dropping the ChapStick in her purse. "What are you going to do over Christmas vacation?"

I think a minute. "My grandmother is coming," I say.

"Oh, that's nice," Virginia says, slipping the strap of

her purse over her shoulder. "My grandmother used to make pfeffernusse at Christmastime. Do you know what that is?"

I shake my head.

"So what's the damage?" Steve asks my father.

"They're heavenly," Virginia says. "They're rolled cookies made with honey and spices and then dusted with confectioners' sugar."

My father clears his throat. He hates discussing money under the best of circumstances. "Two-fifty," he says quickly.

I glance sharply up at him. I know the table has been priced at $400. I've studied the price list, tucked inside each of the two hundred brochures he had printed up on Sweetser's advice. My father hasn't given away more than twenty of them. Sweetser argued with him about the pricing, insisting that my father was quoting figures that were too low.

"These are good," Sweetser said. "How many hours did you put into that table?"

"That's irrelevant," my father said.

"Not irrelevant if you want what's coming to you."

My father won the argument, and he thinks his prices fair now, even modest. My father is living on the money from the sale of the house in New York as well as my parents' savings. Still, though, selling the table for $250 is like giving it away.

"Sold," Steve says.

There is movement then, and tasks, and a discussion about the logistics of fitting the table in the couple's car versus having it sent. In the end it's agreed that my father will have the table shipped collect. Discreetly, Virginia writes a check and lays it on an end table.

We all walk to the back hallway. The couple zip up their parkas and shake my father's hand. "Good seeing you," Steve says.

"Good meeting you," Virginia says to my father and me.

"You know, maybe we could get together," Steve says. "Go out for dinner or have a drink. We're staying at the Woodstock Inn until Friday. How about I give you a call?"

My father nods slowly. "Sure," he says.

"You got something to write on?" Steve asks. "I'll take your number."

My father disappears into the kitchen.

This ought to be good, I am thinking.

"Would you like to see my mural of ski mountains?" I ask on a sudden impulse. Almost no one except my father and grandmother and Jo has seen it.

"Oh, yes, we'd love to," Virginia says. "Where is it?"

"In my bedroom," I say.

I turn and walk, trusting they will follow me. They do, peppering me with questions. Do I like living in Shepherd? Do I miss New York? Do I play any sports at school?

I begin to regret the invitation when I notice the package of toilet paper rolls wedged between the railings on the stairs. I've left a wet towel on the landing, and I can see that the bathroom is a mess, with tissues on the lip of the sink and another towel draped over the toilet. My father and I clean the house on Saturday mornings; by Tuesday it's a mess. I wait for Virginia and Steve to climb the stairs. As we pass my father's room, I have the presence of mind to shut his door, preventing the couple from seeing the unmade bed and the laundry basket on the floor. By the time we reach my bedroom, I deeply regret my stupid idea. I haven't made my bed, my flannel pajamas are on the floor, and there's an empty Ring Ding package on my bedside table. Worse, a pair of underpants is hooked over a chair post.

"Oh, it's fabulous," Virginia says.

"You're quite an artist," Steve says.

"I've never seen anything like it," Virginia says.

"What kind of paint did you use?" Steve asks.

I see the mural then for what it is: a poorly executed and primitive panorama of the three northern New England states, Canada glowing pinkly near the ceiling, *Massachusetts* spelled wrong and ineptly corrected with black paint, the peaks lime-colored where they've been overpainted white to signal that I've skied the mountain.

"You must be quite a skier," Steve says.

"Maybe you and your dad will come skiing with us," Virginia says in a voice I wouldn't use on a three-year-old.

I pocket the underpants.

"Is that a chalet?" Steve asks.

"Oh, look, Steve — Attitash!" Virginia says.

I move toward the doorway.

"You've got your father's talent," Steve says. "Maybe you'll be an architect like he was."

"I'm going down," I say.

"It's a shame he had to give it up." Steve pauses. "Not that the furniture isn't terrific, too."

"Was my dad good at it?" I ask.

"The best," Steve says. "He was a beautiful draftsman. Not all architects are."

"Oh," I say.

"It's probably why his furniture has such a nice line," he adds.

"Beads!" Virginia exclaims. "You make necklaces!"

We meet my father in the back hallway. Steve takes the piece of paper from him and waves it in the air. "I'll give you a call," he says.

I watch the couple walk to their car through the thickening snow. I notice that they don't speak to each other while Steve makes a three-point turn, a dead giveaway they're waiting until they're out of sight. They both smile on cue as they take off down the driveway.

"You finish your glue-up?" I ask my father.

It seems to take a minute for his eyes to focus on mine. "Sort of," he says.

"Did you know him well?" I ask. "I don't remember him from when I visited your office."

"Not very well. He worked in another department."

"She's pretty, don't you think?" I snatch a knitted cap from a hook and start to bat it in the air.

"I guess," he says.

"What did you write on the piece of paper?"

"Just a number."

"Whose?"

"No idea," he says.

I pick up the cap, which has fallen to the floor. "You want a tuna sandwich?" I ask.

"That sounds good."

But still we stand in the hallway, neither of us willing to leave. I notice through the window that it's snowing more heavily now.

"Dad?" I ask, moving closer to him.

"What?"

I put the hat on my head. "Did you like your job when you worked in New York City?"

"I did, Nicky," he says. "Yes, I did."

"Were you good at it? Being an architect?"

"I believe I was."

"What kind of things did you design?"

"Schools. Hotels. Some renovated apartment buildings."

"Will you ever go back to it?" I ask.

He plucks the cap off my head and puts it on his own. "I don't think so," he says.

"Is this going to be a big snow?" I ask.

"Could be," my father says. He looks silly in the hat.

"What a waste," I say. "It's vacation now."

"You just had a snow day," my father says.

"When's Grammie coming?" I ask.

"Tomorrow night."

"Did you get my Christmas present yet?"

"Not telling," he says.

"I was thinking I might like a tape player. Actually, I *need* a tape player."

"Is that so," my father says.

Later that afternoon I am working on a beaded necklace for my grandmother when I hear a motor. I go to the window and look out and see a small blue car in the driveway. I watch as it keeps going to the side of the barn where my father keeps his truck.

Wow, I think. A Christmas rush.

I run down the stairs and open the door. A young woman stands on the doorstep, her hands in the pockets of a pale blue parka. She looks up through her dark blond hair. She pushes the hair off her face and tucks it behind her ear. Her hair is very fine and dead straight.

"Is Mr. Dillon here?" she asks in a voice so faint I have to lean my head out the door.

"Did you say *Dillon?*" I ask.

She nods.

"Yes, he's here."

"A man at the antiques store says Mr. Dillon makes furniture and has some pieces for sale? That I should come up here and take a look? I'm sorry, I didn't know where to park." Her voice is strained, and she speaks in a rush. She has eyes that match her jacket, and her lashes are covered with flakes. The snow is making a lace cap at the top of her head.

"You better come in," I say.

She steps across the threshold. Her jeans fall over her boots and are wet at the hems. She takes a quick glance around the back hallway — at the woolen hats and baseball caps, at the fall and winter jackets, at a bag of road salt and a can of WD-40 on a shelf. It has grown darker with the snow, so I flip on the light switch. The woman flinches slightly with a small twitch of her head. Her hair falls across her face again, and she tucks it behind her ear.

"I'll get my father," I say.

I run along the passageway and into the barn. He looks up from the drawer he's working on.

"You'll never believe this," I say. "We've got another customer."

"I thought I heard a motor," he says.

He returns with me to the house. The woman is still standing by the back door. Her shoulders are hunched, and she has her arms folded across her chest.

"The furniture's in the front room," my father says, gesturing with his hand.

"I should take off my boots," the woman says.

I am about to say that it doesn't matter, but the woman is already unzipping a black leather boot. She shakes it off and then unzips the other. She places them side by side on the mat. The hems of her jeans fall to the floor. When she stands, I can see that her face is pasty — not unusual in the winter in New Hampshire.

"I need something for my parents for Christmas," she says.

"I can show you what I have," my father says. He glances through the window. "You have any trouble with the road?" he asks.

"It's pretty slippery," she says.

I follow my father and the woman into the front room. Her parka flares at her hips. Her hair is caught in the back of her collar. She moves stiffly, and I'm guessing she's wishing that she hadn't come.

In the front room the light is such that my father and I can see what we didn't just an hour earlier: the cherry and walnut and maple tables and chairs are covered with a fine layer of dust.

"Let me get a cloth," my father says.

When he leaves the room, the woman frees her hair from her collar. She unzips her parka. I examine her clothes. She has on a pink cardigan over a white blouse that she hasn't tucked into her jeans. At her throat is a silver amulet on a leather cord. I make beaded necklaces on fine rawhide with silver clasps. I plan to sell them in the summer with the raspberries.

"I like your necklace," I say.

"Oh," she says, her hand going to her throat. "Thanks."

"I make jewelry," I add.

"That's great," she says in a voice that makes it clear she isn't thinking about jewelry.

She fingers a table, leaving a meandering trail in the dust.

"So you need a present," I say.

"Yes," she says. "For my parents."

"Do you live in Shepherd?" I ask, pretty sure I haven't seen her in town.

"I'm just shopping," she says.

"Sorry about this," my father says as he returns with a dustcloth.

The woman stands to one side as he polishes the table. "Your stuff is nice," she says.

She wanders from piece to piece, touching each one as she passes by. She rubs her fingers along the back of a chair and touches the side of a bookcase. She keeps glancing at my father. "Maybe they'd like a bookcase," she says. I think she's going to add something else, but then she shuts her mouth. She has a full face, though she doesn't seem especially fat. Her eyes look wrong, though, as if they belonged in a different face, an unhealthy face maybe. There are bluish half-moons beneath her lower lids.

I decide she's too embarrassed to ask about prices, so I volunteer the list. "We have a price list," I say.

My father gives a quick shake of his head.

The woman tosses her hair out of her face. "Yes," she says. "Sure."

Ignoring my father I take a pamphlet from the mantel and hand it to her. I watch as she reads it. "What's this made of?" she asks my father, pointing to a small cabinet.

"It's walnut," my father answers, failing to add that it has paneled doors, inset hinges, and a beeswax finish as well. He's hopeless as a salesman.

The woman walks around to the back of the chair. She puts a hand out and leans on it. "This is really beautiful," she says.

She takes a step sideways and catches the hem of her jeans under her foot. She bends and rolls the hem into a cuff. I watch her as she does this. She rolls the other pant leg and stands, but I am still looking at her feet. In the moment that my mind registers the socks with the cable knit up the side — pearl-gray angora socks — she says to my father, "I didn't come here to buy a piece of furniture."

My father looks confused for a moment. He thinks her a reporter, come to interview him under false pretenses.

"I don't understand," he says.

But I do, and how is that? The socks, of course, with their angora cable, frayed slightly at the heel. I see it in her face as well, even though I shouldn't be able to see — I'm too young; I'm only twelve — the puffiness, the bluish commas under the eyes, the skin like something wet.

Her hand on the chair presses down, and I worry that she'll fall. "I've come to thank you," she says to my father.

"For what?" my father asks.

And now it's she who seems surprised. "For finding the baby," she says, her voice light on the word *baby*, as if she hardly dared to say it, as if she might not be allowed to say it now.

But still my father, who always seems to understand everything, doesn't understand.

"For finding her," she repeats.

He frowns and gives a quick shake of his head.

I whisper to him, "*The mother,*" and his head shoots back in sudden comprehension.

"You're the mother?" he asks, astonished.

Her cheeks pinken, making her eyes look as blue as the fish I once painted in Clara's bedroom.

The snow at the windows makes no sound. The woman's hand, on the rung of the chair, is as white as a pearl.

"You're the mother of the infant who was left in the snow?" he asks.

"Yes," the woman says, pressing her lips tightly together.

"I'm going to have to ask you to leave," my father says.

"I just wanted to say —"

"Save it," he says curtly.

She is silent, but she doesn't move.

"You can't be here," my father says. "You left a baby to die in the snow."

"I need to see the place," she says.

"What place?"

"Where you found her," she says.

My father seems bewildered by her request. "You ought to know the place."

But how can she know the place where her child was left to die, I want to ask, if she didn't take the baby there herself? Wasn't it the detective who said it was a man who put the baby in a sleeping bag?

"I should never have come," the woman says. "I'll go now."

"Please," my father says.

The woman begins to zip up her jacket. She moves sideways around the furniture.

"You should leave this area," my father says. "They're looking for you."

"I know," she says.

"Then what are you doing here?" he asks.

"Will you turn me in?" she asks.

"I don't even know your name."

"Do you want to know it?" she asks, offering herself up to my father, to this stranger, to this man to whom she owes everything.

"I don't even want to know you exist," my father says.

The woman shuts her eyes, and I think that she will fall. I take a step forward and then stop — too young, of course, to be of help.

"Do you have any idea what you've done?" he asks.

"It wasn't . . ." she begins.

I am certain she was about to say, *It wasn't me,* and apparently my father thinks so, too. "You were there, weren't you?" he asks.

"Yes," she says.

"Don't say another word," my father says as he turns to me. "Nicky, leave the room."

"Dad," I say.

The woman's knees go first, and she seems about to squat. She thrusts her arms forward, but she takes the corner of the table with her chin. I have never seen a real person faint. It's not like in the movies or in books. It's ugly, and it's frightening.

My father kneels beside the woman, and he lifts her head off the floor. She comes to almost immediately and seems not to know where she is. "Nicky, get me a glass of water," my father says.

Reluctantly I leave the room. My hands are trembling as I turn the faucet on. I fill the glass nearly to the brim, and it spills a bit as I run with it to the den. When I get there, the woman is sitting up.

"What happened?" she asks.

"You fainted," my father says. "Here, drink this." He hands her the glass of water. "Can you make it to the car? We have to get you to the hospital."

Her hand is so fast I barely see it. It snakes around and clutches my father's wrist. "I can't," she says, looking at him. "I won't." Her face is pale, almost green. "I'm leaving," she says, letting go of my father's wrist. "I shouldn't have come. I'm sorry." She makes an effort to stand. Beads of sweat have popped onto her forehead.

"Sit down," my father says, and after a second's hesitation, she does. "When did you last eat?"

"If you take me to the hospital," she says, "they'll arrest me."

A simple truth. They will.

The woman bends over and vomits onto her jeans.

My father puts a hand on her back. I can hardly believe what I am seeing. The fainting, the vomiting — it's all wrong in our house.

"Nicky," my father says, "get me a wet paper towel and a pot."

In the kitchen I rip a wad of paper towel from the holder and wet it. I find a saucepan in a cabinet. When I return I hand the woman the paper towels so that she can clean herself up. I'm shaking as I set the pot on the floor.

The woman wipes her jeans. She leans against the leg of the table. "I need a bathroom," she says. With effort, she makes it to her feet. She begins to sway. My father reaches for her arm and catches her.

"Steady now," he says.

Together, my father and the woman move to the back hallway, where the bathroom is. I watch as she detaches herself, enters the bathroom, and closes the door.

Agitated, my father runs his hands through his hair. "This is a disaster," he says.

"You can't take her to the hospital," I say.

"She needs medical help."

"Maybe she hasn't eaten. Maybe she's just tired."

"She can't stay here."

"But Dad . . ."

My father and I stand between the kitchen and the bathroom, near enough to hear the woman if she calls out but not so close that we can listen to whatever is going on behind the door. My father puts his hands in his pockets and jiggles the change there. Each of us is silent then, absorbing the fact of the woman who has entered our house, who has, however briefly, entered our lives. My father walks to the back door, opens it, gazes out at the snow, and shuts the door. He crosses his arms in front of his chest again.

"Christ," he says.

I climb the stairs and head for my room. On a shelf in my closet behind a duffel bag, I find a pair of pajamas my grandmother made for me. I hate them and wanted to throw them out, but my father insisted that I keep them to wear when my grandmother comes to visit. They have childish pink and blue bears on them and a big elastic waist.

When I return, my father is in the kitchen. He has lit a cigarette. The smoke rises and makes a quick left turn in a draft from the window. We hover, my father with his cigarette and I with my flannel bundle, as if waiting to be called upon to save the young woman in the bathroom. First the infant and now the mother.

The door opens and the woman's head pokes through. She looks at my father and then at me. "Can I speak to you?" she asks.

I point to myself, a question on my face.

"Yes, please," she says.

I walk to the door.

"Do you have a Kotex?" she whispers.

A Kotex, I am thinking. Oh God, a Kotex.

"No," I say, chagrined.

"None?" She seems surprised.

"No."

She tilts her head. "How old are you?"

"Twelve."

I have a pad that the school nurse gave each of the seventh-grade girls at the beginning of the school year *just in case,* but it's in my locker. "I'm sorry," I say, and I truly am. I'm more than sorry — I'm mortified.

The woman looks out the window at the falling snow. "It's bad out there, isn't it?"

I offer up the flannel pajamas.

"What's this?" she asks.

"Pajamas," I say. "They're too big for me. The waist is elastic."

Her arms slide through the gap, and I see that her legs are naked. She glances out the window again. "Maybe there's something?" she adds as she shuts the door.

I return to the kitchen and lean against the red counter.

How am I ever going to manage this? I wonder. I close my eyes and think a minute.

"Dad?" I say finally. "I need to go to Remy's." My tone is slightly defiant, anticipating an argument.

"Remy's," my father says, stubbing out his cigarette in a saucer he keeps for the purpose.

"I have to get something."

"What?"

I shrug.

"Something for you or something for her?" he asks.

"Something for her," I say.

"What is it?"

"Something for her," I repeat.

My father gets up and walks to the window again. He examines the snow, gauging depth and speed. The tracks of his truck and the blue car are nearly covered now.

"It's *important*," I add.

"There's nothing else that will do?" he asks.

"No," I say.

"You're sure?" he says.

Yes, there might be a cloth or a towel that would do, but I have never before been given such a mission, and I am determined not to fail this woman. "*Please,* Dad," I say.

"I'll go," he says. "You stay here." But as he says this, I can see him reconsidering. He doesn't want me in the house alone with the woman.

"Never mind," he says. "You'll come with me."

*   *   *

We dress in silence for the snow. I tap on the door and tell the woman we're going to the store and that we'll be right back. We climb into the truck, and my father starts the engine. He steps out and scrapes the snow from the windshield and the windows. I tell myself it isn't so bad out, but it is: the snow is falling fast and thick.

Our road, unplowed, is slippery beneath the wheels of the truck. My father drives with concentration, and we don't speak.

I wonder if he's thinking the same thing I am — that we just left a strange woman in our house, a woman who may have tried to murder her baby. *Murder her baby.* I cannot make the phrase sit still in my head. Since we moved to New Hampshire, nothing ever happens to my father and me; hardly anyone ever drives up the long hill. But in the past nine days, we've had three sets of visitors: Detective Warren, Steve and Virginia, and now a woman whose name we still do not know.

We pass the school and the church and the village green. At the corner of Strople and Maine, the rear wheels of the truck begin to float across the street. My father takes his hands off the steering wheel, and after what feels like many seconds, we come to a stop. My father puts the truck in gear and pulls into our lane. I'm praying that we don't hit something, because if we do it will be all my fault.

Up ahead I can see both Remy's and Sweetser's, but my father makes a sudden turn into the post office. I guess he wants to check his mail. Instead of stopping at the post office, however, he pulls behind that building to another building that houses both the police station and the town clerk's office.

"What are you doing?" I ask, my eyes widening.

My father doesn't answer me. He parks the truck, turns the engine off, and opens his door.

"Dad?" I ask.

I watch my father walk toward the police station. I open my door and hop out. Did he intend to come here all along? Did he agree to go to the store simply to get me out of the house while the police arrest the mother of the baby? Would my father do that? I'm not sure. Sometimes I think I know my father very well; at other times I wonder if I know him at all. "Dad!" I yell, running after him.

My father stops at the door and waits for me to catch up to him. He bends toward me. In a quiet voice that I know means business, he says, *"Go back to the truck."*

"What are you doing?"

"This has nothing to do with you."

"But you can't . . . ," I say, holding my hands out. "You just can't." Already I feel a sense of loyalty to a woman I don't even know. I shake my head vigorously back and forth.

My father feels a nudge at his back. He steps aside so that the door can open. Peggy, the town clerk, pulls a scarf around her head. "Hi, Nicky," she says, stepping outside.

I first met Peggy when I applied for a permit to sell raspberries at the end of our road. She charged me seven dollars.

Peggy smiles at my father. "You need me?" she asks.

"Actually I'm looking for Chief Boyd," my father says.

"You just missed him," she says. "He and Paul got called out to eighty-nine. An accident at the exit." Peggy looks at the sky. "Is it urgent? I could raise him on the radio."

I stare at my father.

"No," he says after a few seconds. "No, that's all right. I'll give him a call."

I let out a long breath.

"Well, you've certainly been in the news," Peggy says, pulling on her gloves. "What a thing that must have been!" she says. "To find a baby." She looks at me. "And you were with him, too!"

I nod.

"I'm off to Sweetser's," Peggy says. "Have to get some batteries and road salt before the storm gets worse. You want to wait inside? I won't lock the door."

"No, we're fine," my father says. "Thanks."

"If I don't see you later, have a good Christmas," Peggy says.

My father and I walk to the truck. I climb into the cab.

I know enough not to ask a single question, not to say a word.

At Remy's my father slows to the curb. Through the whiteout and the steamed window, I can see the pale yellow light of a bulb above the register. My father hands me a ten-dollar bill. "Make it snappy," he says.

The steps are poorly shoveled. A bell rings when I enter the store, needlessly announcing me. Marion sets her knitting down. "Nicky," she says. "Sweetheart. You're my hero, you know that? Haven't seen you since you found the baby. Haven't seen your dad either."

"We've been kind of busy," I say.

"Well, I guess so!"

Marion, a large redhead with a rubbery face, married her sister's husband after an affair of biblical proportions that shocked even the most ardent proponents of New Hampshire's highly unrealistic state motto, *Live Free or Die.* But that was years ago, and now the woman is a pillar of the community. Her husband, Jimmy, who was once the Regional's star quarterback, weighs in at over three hundred pounds. One of Marion's sons is at UNH; the other is at the state prison for armed robbery.

I have hardly ever seen Marion without knitting needles in her hands. Today she's making something in red and yellow stripes. I hope it's not for anyone over two years old. "So tell me all about it!" she says.

"Um," I say, thinking.

"Something that wasn't in the papers."

I think another moment. "We wrapped her in flannel shirts and put her in a plastic laundry basket."

"You did?" Marion says, seemingly happy with the detail. "Were you just completely freaked out?"

"Pretty much," I say.

Marion picks up her knitting. "You went to the hospital, too?"

"I did."

"Did you get to stay with the baby?"

"We visited for a minute."

"What's going to happen to her?"

"We don't really know," I say.

Marion loses her rubbery smile. "It's sad," she says.

"Well, we did find her," I say, not yet willing to relinquish the role of heroine.

"No, I mean sad for the person who did it," she says. "There must have been a terrible reason."

I think about how the person who did it is in our bathroom at home right this minute.

"You finish the hat for your dad?"

"Yes," I say, inching closer to the aisles.

"How did it come out?"

"Pretty good," I say. "I think it'll fit him."

"You ended up liking the rolled edge?"

"I did," I say.

My mother taught me how to knit when I was seven. I forgot about knitting until one day I saw Marion at the counter with hers and confessed that I knew how. Confessed is the right word. In those days, in the early 1980s, knitting was not a hobby a preteen would readily admit to. But Marion, ever enthusiastic, pounced upon me and insisted that I show her something I'd made. I did — a misshapen scarf — which she praised extravagantly. She lent me a raspberry-colored wool for another project, a hat for myself. Since then I've been knitting pretty continuously. It's addictive and it's soothing, and for a few minutes anyway, it makes me feel closer to my mother. When I run into trouble with a particular stitch or a pattern, I go down to the store, and Marion helps me sort it out. Usually, I am fascinated by whatever Marion is knitting, by the way a ball of string can become a sweater or a baby blanket, but today I just want to get away from the counter as fast as I can. I think of my father waiting in the car, about the way the snow must be covering the windshield already.

I know where the feminine products are kept, and I move in that direction. The box of Kotex seems larger than I imagined it would be. I take it down from the shelf and return to the counter.

Marion sets her knitting on her lap. "Oh, my," she says, looking at the Kotex.

Foolishly, recklessly, I blurt, "It's not for me."

Marion tilts her head and smiles a maternal smile. It's clear she doesn't believe me.

I take the ten-dollar bill from my pocket. The Kotex pulses and sings a tune on the scuffed Formica. Marion punches prices into the register. "You feeling okay?" she asks.

"I'm just fine," I say.

"You know, if you have any questions about anything, anything at all, you can always ask me."

I nod. My face is hot.

"You not having, you know, your mother around," she says lightly.

I bite my lip. I just want to leave.

"Not too many people in today," Marion says. "But yesterday you should have seen the rush for milk and canned goods. Stocking up. It's supposed to be a big storm. Biggest of the season, they're saying, but they're always wrong."

I put the money on the counter.

"Have you seen the baby since that night?" Marion asks, making my change.

"No."

Marion looks up quickly, and behind me there's a voice. "Nicky, isn't it?"

A blue overcoat and a red muffler slide beside me. I didn't hear the bell announcing Detective Warren's arrival. Well, maybe there wasn't a bell, I realize; maybe he was already in the store, in another aisle.

"How are you?" he asks.

"Fine," I say through tight lips.

Marion slips the Kotex into a paper bag, but not before Warren has surely seen my purchase. Sweat blossoms inside my parka. I stand as though I'm not really there — head slightly bent, back hunched. Warren puts his magazines and a package of gum on the counter.

"I'm going now," I say.

"Camels," Warren says.

"Have a good Christmas," Marion calls to me. "And tell your dad I think he's a hero, too."

"Yes, you and your dad have a good holiday," Warren says.

I walk as fast as I dare to the door. All I can think about is what will happen if my father sees the detective.

The bell rings as I open it. I slip and skid off the top step and take the rest on my butt. I pick myself up and run to the truck.

I slam the door and throw my head back against the seat. There's snow in the paper bag. "Let's go quick," I say. "I have to pee."

The ride back to the house is tense and long. At times my father has trouble finding the road. Again and again I feel the sway of the rear tires skidding out or jumping a rut. We see only a couple of other vehicles on the roads — few willing, it seems, to venture out in the storm.

We pass the small white cottage with its evidence of boys. I rub the condensation from the truck window and strain to see inside. The house has candles in the windows. I can see a lit tree in a living room. The mother is in the kitchen near a counter. She has her hair pulled back into a ponytail. Fragments of Christmas memories float across my vision:

She puts the baby ornament on the tree.

The ribbon on the package is bright red, curled with a rip from the scissors.

He is on his knees, his head beneath the branches, looking for the socket.

I am thinking about Christmas trees and ornaments when I have a sudden realization: Did I really tell Marion the Kotex wasn't for me? Did the detective, lurking in the aisles, hear that?

Stupid, stupid, stupid.

My father parks in his usual spot at the far side of the barn. I look at the woman's blue car as I open the door and head for the house. I find her sitting on the bench in the back hallway. She has on her white shirt and the bottoms of my flannel pajamas. They barely fit — the thighs tight with pink and blue animals, the cuffs just inches below her knees. Her legs are white to the tops of her gray angora socks. Her jeans, which she has washed, hang on a hook, drying.

She looks chastened and subdued, a student waiting outside the principal's office. I hand her the paper bag. She says thank you and slips inside the bathroom. I take off my jacket and hang it on a hook not far from the one that holds her jeans.

Beyond the bathroom door, I hear a rip of cardboard, the rustle of paper.

The woman has had a baby. What does it feel like? I want to ask. I know where babies come from, but that doesn't tell me what I crave to understand. Does it hurt?

Was she frightened? Does she love the man who is the father? Is he waiting out of sight down the road for her to return? Is the ridiculously named Baby Doris the result of a grand passion? Does the woman behind the bathroom door cry for her lover and her lost child?

The woman emerges from the bathroom looking more careworn than passionate. We stand for a moment in the back hallway, and I'm not sure what to do with her. "Thank you," she says again. "Was it bad out?"

"It was fine."

My father brings a wave of cold air with him as he stomps the snow off his boots. He slips his sleeves from his jacket and puts it on a hook. "You should lie down," he says to the woman.

I lead her past the kitchen and into the den. I point to the couch. She falls onto the sofa in a kind of loose collapse. Her stomach swells over the elastic band of the pajamas, visible where the white shirt parts at the waist. The shirt isn't clean: rings of dust, like fine stitching, run along the inside edges of the cuffs. She lies with her eyes closed, and I examine her, this prize.

Her lips are dry, and she wears no makeup, a minor disappointment. Her eyebrows have been expertly plucked, however, suggesting prior care and grooming. Her eyelashes are thick and blond. There are blackheads on her nose and one or two faint depressions on her cheeks. Her hair falls over her face, and I think she must have fallen asleep already not to mind its touch on her skin. Her breasts are large and list toward the couch cushion.

I wait, as one might beside a mother's bed, for her to wake up or to open her eyes. In the kitchen I can hear the electric whine of a can opener, the scrape of a saucepan against a burner. I cover her with an ugly black-and-red crocheted blanket my grandmother made and which my father refuses to throw out. I plump the pillows behind her head, hoping this will rouse her, and it does.

She sits up quickly, once again as if not knowing where she is — the beauty in the fairy tale who has slept a thousand years.

"I've left him," the woman says.

I sit up straighter. Left *him?* The *man?* The one who took the baby into the snow?

She shivers.

"You're cold," I say. "I'll get your jacket."

"My sweater's in the bathroom."

I am up in an instant, eager to be of use. I find the folded pink cardigan on a corner of the sink. It's made of a fleecy wool — not angora but mohair — and has large mother-of-pearl buttons down the front.

When I return the woman lifts herself up. I wrap the cardigan around her shoulders, trying to tug it down. She seems to have lost the use of her arms, and her body is heavy.

I sit on the floor next to her. The room is filled with bookcases that tower over us. Besides the couch there are only the two lamps, a coffee table, the leather club chair my father saved from our New York house, and one other chair. My father comes in with a tray: Chicken with Stars in a bowl, a fan of saltines hastily arranged on a plate, a glass of water. "You're dehydrated," he says, studying her.

She brings herself up to a sitting position. Her hand is shaky as she holds the spoon.

"As soon as the storm stops . . . ," he says, gesturing toward the window.

As soon as the storm stops, *what?* I'd like to know. Wrestle the woman to the truck? Make her drive her blue car down an unplowed road?

My father sits and assumes his usual position: head bent, legs spread, his elbows on his knees. The room darkens, and my father reaches over to turn on the lamp. "How did you find me?" he asks.

"I read about you in the newspaper," she says. "Your name was there. It was easy enough to find out where you live."

Beyond the windows the snow falls in fat flakes. "Have you seen a doctor?" he asks.

She looks up.

"While you were pregnant," he adds.

"No."

"You never saw a doctor?"

"No," she says again.

"That was foolish," my father says.

She opens her mouth to speak, but he holds up his hand, cutting her off. "I don't want to know," he says, standing. "Nicky, I want you to start shoveling."

"Now?" I ask.

"Yes, now," he says. "I have to go over to the barn and finish that bureau."

"But —"

"No buts. If we don't keep up with the storm, we'll never get out of here."

I stand reluctantly with a parting glance at the woman on the couch. She doesn't look up at me. I drag myself to the back hallway, sit on the bench, and put on my boots. What if she needs me? I think. I put on my jacket and hat and mittens. Should she be left alone? I go outside and bend my head against the snow. What if something happens to her and I'm not there?

I use a wide shovel and push it forward like a plow. Of all my chores I hate shoveling the most, particularly when it's snowing and it's clear that in a couple of hours I'll have to do it all over again. I make rows, pushing the snow to the far edge of the top of the driveway. I'm impatient, and I do this in record time. After twenty minutes, I survey my work. It's sloppy, but I can't bear to be outside a minute longer. I lean the shovel by the back door, step inside, and undress quickly. I walk to the den.

The woman is still sitting on the couch with the tray on her lap. She has left the stars to float in an oily golden puddle at the bottom of the bowl. I always eat the stars first. She leans over to set the tray aside, but I take it from her. Clara Barton. Florence Nightingale.

Again she lies down. The light from the lamp falls on her hair and her face. I sit once again on the floor and lay my arm against the piping on the cushions. "What's your name?" I ask.

"Your father doesn't want to know," she says. "You're not supposed to be in here."

"I won't tell him," I say.

She says nothing.

"We have to call you *something*," I point out.

The woman thinks a minute. Two minutes. "You can call me Charlotte," she says finally.

"Charlotte?" I ask.

She nods.

Charlotte, I repeat silently. I don't know any Charlottes, have never known a Charlotte. "It's a pretty name," I say. "Is it your real name?"

"It is," she says.

I want to know so much then. How old is she? Where is she from? Who is the man? Did she love him very much?

"The baby's doing fine," I say instead.

Sobs — a gulp, a second gulp — escape her. Her eyes scrunch up and snot runs down her upper lip. She is not a delicate crier. She wipes her nose with a pink sleeve. I run to the bathroom and come back with a wad of toilet paper.

"I'm sorry," I say. "I shouldn't have said anything."

She waves my apology away.

"Tell me about it," I plead.

"I can't," she says, blowing her nose. "Not now."

But the *now* is everything, isn't it? *Now* implies a future, a time when she will confide in me and tell me her tale — if only I can wait, if only I can be patient. I am dizzy with the promise of the word.

"I think I really need to sleep," she says, giving her nose a final tidying.

"We have a guest room," I say. "For my grandmother. She's coming for Christmas. You can close the door and sleep there."

"Your father won't mind?"

"No," I say with no authority whatsoever.

She rises up from the couch, sloughing off the sweater and the throw. I lead her to the back stairs. She walks haltingly and uses the banister to pull herself up. She follows me to a room with a double bed covered with a white spread that used to be on my parents' bed years ago. I take a quilt from the closet and lay it as best I can over the coverlet. Beside the bed is a small table with a lamp on it, and to its right a bureau with a mirror. In another corner is a rocking chair, and beside that an especially bright lamp that my father set up so that my grandmother can sit and read when she visits. The woman moves directly to the bed, draws back the covers, and lies down at once.

"I'll come back in a while and see if you're all right," I say.

The woman's eyes are closed, and she seems already to have fallen asleep.

Reluctantly I turn and leave. I shut the door with exaggerated care. I sit on the bottom step for a time — for the time it would take to give the area nearest to the house a really good shoveling — and then I walk over to the barn.

"I've put her in the guest room," I say.

My father stands back from the table saw. "I don't want you talking to her," he says, lowering his safety goggles. "I thought I made that clear."

I shrug.

"As soon as this lets up, I'm going to insist that she leave. You can't be part of this, Nicky."

"You mean *you* can't be part of this."

"No, I mean *you*," he says, pointing a finger. "This is serious business. And you're not to say a word to anyone. Not now. Not ever. Do you understand?"

I turn and leave my father's shop before he can get going on a lecture. I fetch the tray from the den, take it into the kitchen, and wash the dishes. I finish off the soup, spooning it directly from the saucepan. I climb the stairs and stand outside the guest room, listening for a telltale sound, any sound with which to weave a story. Disappointed, I walk into my room and sit at my desk and try to work on the beaded necklace for my grandmother — a complicated and ambitious project with a sculpted pendant — but I am jumpy and can't make my fingers do what I want them to do. From time to time I move to the window and look out at the snow and am comforted by the whiteout and the wind that has come up, signaling a blizzard. Clothes might be a problem, I am thinking, but she can wear my father's shirts. Her jeans will dry soon enough. Fitful, I lie on my bed and stare up at the ceiling and imagine a week during which Charlotte will stay with us. I see the two of us sitting in various cozy positions, my father conveniently gone, while she tells me her fabulous and lurid tale.

I sit up. I have an idea.

I collect the hair dryer from the upstairs bathroom and take it downstairs. I lift the jeans from the hook in the back hallway and hang them instead on the hook on the back of the bathroom door. The jeans are wet all along the inner thighs. I hold out the legs and aim the dryer the way I've had to do with T-shirts, the ones that come back from the Laundromat slightly damp because of my father's impatience to "get going."

The heavy denim takes longer to dry than I think it should, and I hope I'm not waking Charlotte with the sound. I don't want her to catch me doing this; I simply want her to find her clothes warm and nicely folded.

When I turn off the hair dryer, I hear knocking at the back door.

Another customer? *Impossible,* I think. We barely got up the road ourselves.

I step out of the bathroom and see a flash of red in the window of the door. I freeze in place, like a statue in a child's game. I suck in my breath. I have no choice but to walk forward and open the door.

"Nicky," Warren says, stepping inside.

There's a staccato of stomped feet, snow falling to the floor. "Your father around?" he asks.

A silent screech rings in my ear. "No," I say.

"I just had one or two questions for him," Warren says, beginning to melt on the welcome mat. "I wanted to get over here before the storm does its worst."

For a moment I can't speak.

"Where is he?" Warren asks, studying me.

"Um . . . he had to go into the woods to find his ax," I say. "He left it in the woods. He wanted to find it before it gets buried in the snow."

I feel dizzy. The lie is huge. Magnificent.

"Really," Warren says. He opens his coat and shakes it out, a winged bird.

From the back hallway, through the kitchen, I have a view of the den, the couch, and the ugly red-and-black crocheted throw.

"Wicked out there," Warren says.

A pink mohair sweater with mother-of-pearl buttons is lying against the pillows. It is spread open, as if a woman had just risen from it.

Warren wipes his feet a dozen times on the mat. "Could I get a glass of water?" he asks, looking over at the coats on the hooks.

"Um. Sure," I say.

He walks with me to the kitchen. He glances up the stairs as he goes. "I've got snow tires, but even so," he says.

In the kitchen he studies the dishes in the dish drainer. I fetch a glass from the cabinet, fill it from the tap, and hand it to him. I can smell spearmint on his breath. I try not to look at his scar.

"We found a flashlight," he says. "Wanted to know if it was your father's or if it belonged to the guy."

"It's probably my father's," I say quickly. "We lost one in the snow that night."

"Thought it might be," Warren says, looking over my head toward the den. "You put your tree up yet?"

"We'll do it Christmas Eve," I say.

Warren takes a long swallow. "How old are you again?" he asks.

"Twelve," I say.

I hear the back door open. "Dad," I say, looking just past the detective.

I am dead.

"What's going on?" my father asks. The vertical lines on his forehead are pronounced.

"Came to see if you lost a flashlight the night you found the baby," Warren says. "You find your ax?"

My father says nothing.

"Remember, Dad, how you said you were going into the woods to find your ax?" I say, meeting his eyes.

"We found a flashlight," Warren says. "Nicky said you lost one that night."

"I did."

"What brand?"

"Don't know. Black with a yellow switch."

"Yeah, the same," Warren says.

I let a hand fall to just below my waist. I shut my eyes and wince slightly, the way I've seen the girls at school do, as if waiting for a cramp to pass.

"So you guys getting ready for Christmas?"

My father unzips his jacket.

"We got our tree up already," Warren says, taking a sip of water. "One of my boys — the eight-year-old; he's autistic — likes having it up."

My father nods.

"There's a specialist in Concord," Warren says. "Supposed to be the best in New Hampshire. It's why we moved into the city."

I hear a slight creak along the upstairs hallway. I glance at Warren to see if he has heard it, too.

From a hook I snatch a rag and begin to skate with the cloth, drying the floor, the way my father is always trying to get me to do.

"Still, though," Warren is saying, "hard on my wife, hard on Mary. Tommy, that's my son, he doesn't like being touched."

A murmur from my father. A pause and then another string of words. I skate my way to the bottom of the stairs and glance up. Charlotte, her face creased with sleep, is on the upstairs landing.

"We've got a clan coming," Warren is saying. "We'll have nineteen, twenty anyway, for Christmas Eve."

With a quick glance to see that Warren isn't looking, I shake my head once, an emphatic *No.*

"Mary and her sister will do up three hundred pierogies," Warren is saying. "My wife's Polish."

I pick up the rag and reach forward to wipe a step. Silently I beg Charlotte to understand.

Her head tilts then, and I see the way her eyes begin to listen, the moment that she registers the foreign voice. She holds her arms out like a ballerina, and I think for a moment she might fly off the top step. Pirouetting on her toes, she retreats from the landing.

Very carefully, I step away from the stairs. I let out a long breath.

Through the window I can see that the snow has turned icy. It pings against the glass.

"I'll bring you some," Warren is saying. He sets the water glass on a shelf. "Looking bad out there. Better get yourself another flashlight."

"Plenty where that came from," my father says.

"You could lose your power in this," Warren says.

"We could."

The detective glances my way as he pushes open the door against an inch of snow. Warren gives a small wave and bends into the storm, holding his overcoat closed with one hand. He trudges, collar up, across the drive. He wipes the snow off his windshield with his gloves and climbs into his Jeep. As he does he glances at the muffled maze of tracks in the snow. The truck and the blue car cannot be seen from where he is standing. He would have to walk further toward the woods to get the right angle. He does not. I watch him reverse, make the turn, and finally leave.

My father shuts the door. "What on earth do you think you're doing?" he says to me.

I stare at the floor.

"You're going to get us in more trouble than we're in already."

I look up. "I was just trying to get rid of him," I say.

This is true and not entirely true.

"She came to the top of the stairs," I add.

"I know she did. I heard."

"You heard?"

"Yes."

"Do you think he heard?"

"I don't know," my father says. "But I hope for your sake he didn't."

My father closes his jacket with an angry zip. "I'll be in the barn," he says.

The day we left New York, my father packed up a trailer with boxes and tools and suitcases, bicycles and skis and books. He tied a blue plastic tarp over all of it, bent his head to the plastic, and stood for so long I wondered if he'd fallen asleep.

All that morning I'd been expected to help with the packing. The movers would come to get the larger items after we left. My father had put me in the kitchen with a stack of old newspapers and a dozen fresh cardboard boxes and had asked me to see to the dishes. But I was lost in the fatigue of anger and inertia: I didn't want to be packing up to leave. I would lift an item up and look at it and set it down and then pick it up again and think, How am I supposed to pack a pressure cooker? What do I do with a Cuisinart? My legs hurt, my arms hurt, my head hurt from crying. *This is the last time I'll ever see my hallway at night,* I'd been saying to myself for the last twenty-four hours. *This is the last time I'll ever sit on my swing. This is the last time I'll ever reach for the Cheerios in this particular cabinet.* Leaving was a weight upon the entire house and its contents, so that it seemed a Herculean task simply to lift a glass. I packed indifferently, tumblers and plates in the same box, more plates in another box, and I forgot to label the cartons. For months after we moved into the new house, we had to unpack six or seven boxes to find the toaster or the measuring cups or the wooden spoons.

I wouldn't go when my father said it was time to get into the car. He let me be for an hour as he checked and rechecked rooms and closets, looking into cabinets and under beds. In the end, he had to take me bodily from the only home I'd ever known, the one that still had surfaces my mother and Clara had touched. I sobbed all the way to the Massachusetts Turnpike.

The drive from New York to New Hampshire can be done in three hours, but it seemed to take far longer than that to reach our destination. My father drove up Route 91, the highway that runs between New Hampshire and Vermont, not even knowing which state we'd eventually settle in. Exhausted, he stopped in White River Junction, where we ordered a late-night supper neither of us could eat. We asked directions to the nearest motel, where I fell onto my bed fully clothed, meaning to get up and brush my teeth and undress, but I never did. I woke the next morning disoriented and dirty. I felt as though I'd slipped through a hole in time, caught between life as it had been and life as it would be. I had no enthusiasm for the future, and I knew my father didn't either.

In the morning I whined all through the blueberry pancakes, and my father left the diner in disgust. When I finally got into the car, he tried to find his way out of White River Junction in order to continue north. I remember a series of bewildering interchanges, and it was a minute or two before my father realized we were actually heading south on Route 89. "We'll see where this goes," he said, shrugging.

The highway ascended slowly into small mountains with ledges of startling white rock. Waterfalls had frozen blue, and there were still patches of snow on the north sides of the trees and houses. We hadn't gone far — only half an hour — when my father veered off the highway at an exit. Perhaps he realized that if he didn't get off soon, we'd be back in Massachusetts, or maybe he simply needed gas; I can't remember now. We glided off the exit ramp onto Route 10, drove for a mile or two through a small town, and coasted to a stop in front of Croydon Realty.

I was an uncooperative ball in the passenger seat, my arms crossed over my bulky parka, my chin tucked into the collar. I refused even to look at my father.

"Nicky," he said gently.

"*What?*"

"We've got to do our best here," he said.

"Do our best *what?*" I asked.

"Do our best to try to make a go of it," he said.

"I don't want to make a go of it," I said.

He sighed, and I could hear him tapping his fingers against the steering wheel. He waited. "I know how hard this must be for you," he said finally.

"You have no idea," I said, curling myself into an even tighter ball.

"I think I might," he said, his voice deliberately quiet, deliberately calm.

Mine was not. "This is so *unfair!*" I shouted.

"Yes, it is," he said.

"But why?" I wailed.

"There isn't any *why,* Nicky."

"Yes, there is," I said. "We didn't have to leave. We could have stayed at home."

"No, Nicky, we couldn't."

"You mean *you* couldn't."

"That's right. I couldn't."

I began to cry and to shake with the crying. It seemed my natural state then. My father put a hand on my shoulder. I was exhausting both of us. "I'm sorry, Nicky," he said.

I flung his hand off with a twist. I sat up and looked around. "Where are they?" I cried in a sudden panic.

A woman stepped out the door of Croydon Realty. She wound a scarf around her neck. She had on ankle boots with fur on them.

"Where are who?" my father asked.

"You know who," I said. "Mom! And Clara! Where are they?"

"Oh, Nicky," my father said, hopelessly defeated. He shut his eyes and leaned his head back against the headrest.

"I hate you!" I screamed.

I opened my door and stepped out onto the road between the car and the curb. In my fury, I'd forgotten that I'd taken my boots off in the car, as I almost always do, to keep my feet from overheating. I stood in a pile of slush in my stocking feet. The woman on the steps of Croydon Realty paused. My father bent his forehead to the steering wheel.

The woman looked at me and then into the car at my father. She glanced at the trailer with the tarp. She sized us up as a sale. She went back into the office. My ankles ached from the icy water. I hopped back into the car and slammed the door as hard as I could. My father opened his door and stepped out. He adjusted his gray tweed overcoat (the last time he would ever wear it), jumped a puddle, and headed for the Realtor's.

And such was our introduction to Shepherd, New Hampshire.

*　　*　　*

I climb the stairs to the guest room. I knock and call Charlotte's name.

I hear no answer and call her name again. I open the door a crack.

The shades are drawn, and it takes a minute for my eyes to adjust to the gloom. When they do I see that she is sitting in my grandmother's chair. She has her hands folded in her lap, and her posture is rigid.

"Charlotte?"

"You want me to come downstairs," she says evenly.

"No," I say. "No." And I understand that she's been waiting in the silly pajama bottoms to be called downstairs and sent away, possibly even arrested. "No," I say again. "It's just me, Nicky. I've brought you your jeans. And this," I say, holding out the pink sweater.

"Everything's all right?" she asks.

"Everything's fine," I say, and even in the gloom of the room, I can see her shoulders relax.

"Who was it, then?" she asks.

"A detective. His name is Warren. He's the one trying to find you."

"Oh God, I thought so," she says. "How did he know I was here?"

"I don't think he did," I say. "He came to tell my dad

that they'd found a flashlight. . . ." I stop, fearing another collapse. "At the . . . you know," I say quickly.

"Your dad didn't tell him I was here?"

"No."

"Oh God," she says again, but I hear relief and not panic in her voice this time.

"It's okay," I say. "He left. He won't be coming back. Not in this weather."

"I've made you an accomplice," Charlotte says.

Accomplice, I repeat silently. I love the word.

She runs her hand over the pink sweater in her lap.

"You want something to eat?" I ask.

"Not right now."

"I should let you sleep," I say.

"Don't go," she says.

She rises from the chair and sets the jeans and sweater on the cushion. She makes her way to the bed, draws back the covers, and climbs in. It seems such an ordinary gesture in such an ordinary room that I have to remind myself of the awfulness of her crime. Uncertain as to what I should do, I sit on the floor next to the bed, my legs folded beneath me.

"Do you know anything about the baby?" she asks.

I am surprised by the bravery of the question, but I'm afraid to answer it in case she begins again to cry. In the dusk of the bedroom, I can barely see her face. She lies like a child, with her hands tucked under her cheek. I think I can smell her: a warm, yeasty smell, not unsweet.

I take a deep breath and speak rapidly. "She's going to be fine," I say. "Really fine. But she's lost one finger. Her toes and everything else are good, though. I don't know which finger."

"Oh," Charlotte says. It's a small *oh*, not a wail, but a sound that sinks away into the corners.

"She's being cared for by a foster family," I say. I speak carefully now, each word a potentially treacherous step, likely to unleash an avalanche of tears.

"Where?" Charlotte asks.

"We don't know," I say. "I don't think they plan on telling us. They're calling her Baby Doris."

"Doris," she says, clearly surprised.

"We don't know why," I say. "It might be a system they have. You know, like naming hurricanes."

"Doris," she says again, and I can hear a note of indignation in her voice. She sits up a bit.

"That won't be her name . . . you know . . . later," I say.

"Someone will change it," she says.

"Probably."

Charlotte's head falls back against the pillow. "It's an awful name," she says.

"You could get her back," I say quickly. "I'm sure you could get her back."

She doesn't speak.

"Don't you want her back?" I ask.

"I can't take care of her," Charlotte says. Her voice is curiously flat, devoid of emotion. "I have nowhere to live," she adds.

"Nowhere at all?" I ask.

She rolls onto her back and stares at the ceiling. My eyes have adjusted to the dark and I can see her profile: the slightly jutting chin, the lips pressed together, the open eyes, the fabulously long lashes, the smooth forehead. "No," she says.

"You must have lived *somewhere*," I say.

"Well, of course I did," she says. "I just can't go back."

I want to ask *why*, but I tell myself to be careful, to be patient the same way my dad has to be patient when starting up his truck. "How old are you?" I ask instead.

"Nineteen," she says, rolling back toward me. "So it's just you and your father?"

"Yes."

"What happened to your mom?"

"She died," I say.

Charlotte reaches out a hand and touches my shoulder. "I'm so sorry," she says. Her fingers linger a moment longer, and then she draws them back into the covers. "How old were you?"

"I was ten," I say.

"You've had a rough time, haven't you?"

I shrug.

"I had a sister, too," I say. "Her name was Clara. She was a year old. She died with my mom in the car accident."

I expect the hand on the shoulder again, but it stays where it is inside the covers. "What did she look like?" Charlotte asks.

"Clara?"

"Your mom. What did she look like?"

"She was pretty," I say. "Not too tall, but thin. She had long light brown hair that was wavy. She cut it after Clara was born, but I remember her best with it long."

"Like you," Charlotte says. "You'll show me a picture?"

"Yes," I say, "I will." And already I am thinking about the album I have in my room and how Charlotte and I will pore over it.

"I wish I had a picture," she says. "You know, just one picture."

Her wish hits me like a basketball flung at my chest. I realize she probably has no idea what her baby looks like. Was a picture taken in the hospital? Do the police have one on file? "Where did you used to live?" I ask.

"I can't . . . ," she says.

"I won't tell anyone. Not even my father."

"Let's just say it's a small town north of here," she says.

"In New Hampshire?"

"Um, maybe," she says. "Your dad seems like a nice man. He doesn't want me here, and he's angry, but still, he has a nice face. What grade are you in?"

"Seventh," I say.

"Do you like school?"

I shift my legs. "Sort of," I say. The truth is that I do like school, but I don't want to seem too eager in case she thinks anyone who likes school pathetic. It already matters tremendously what Charlotte thinks of me.

"I was in school," she says.

"You were?" I cannot imagine Charlotte behind a desk or reading a book.

"In college," she says. "But I dropped out." She pauses. "I plan to go back, though."

I have the sense then that her entire story — the story I long to hear — is contained within that pause.

"Do you have a boyfriend?" she asks. She moves her head so that it rests at the edge of the bed. I can smell her breath. I have no answer for her. I think of the only friend I have who is a boy, and poor Roger Kelly, he simply doesn't measure up.

"No one yet," I say.

"Oh, you will," she says, and I wonder where her confidence comes from.

I bend my head and pick at the carpet. Now is the moment to ask her about the man. But I hesitate, and in the hesitation I lose the momentum that would make the question easy and natural.

"What's it like outside?" she asks.

"It's pretty bad," I say, looking up. "You'll have to stay

here." I wait for a protest and am heartened when none comes.

"You might have to stay here a couple of days," I say tentatively.

"Oh, I can't stay here a couple of days," she says. She brings her arms out from under the covers. "I didn't mean to stay here at all."

"Where would you have gone?" I ask.

"Oh, I have places," she says vaguely.

Through the shut door and from the bottom of the stairway, I can hear my father calling my name. I unfold my legs and stand up quickly. I don't want him to come upstairs and find me sitting beside Charlotte's bed in a darkened room. "I have to go now," I say. "He's calling me."

"He doesn't want you in here," she says. She props herself up on one elbow. "Thank you for drying my jeans," she adds.

"You can come downstairs when you're ready," I say.

"I shouldn't have come here," she says, gazing at the dull threads of light around the shade at the window.

"I'm glad you did," I blurt out.

"What was it like?" she asks. "When you found her?"

I realize then that I know something she doesn't, and the knowledge seems unearned. I hear my father call my name again. In a minute he will climb the stairs looking for me.

"She was a little messy," I say. "But her eyes were amazing. She seemed so calm, like she was waiting for us. She had dark hair."

"A lot of babies have dark hair at first," Charlotte says. "It falls out. I read about that."

"She was beautiful," I say.

I brace myself for an animal moan — a cow lowing for its calf; a lioness searching for her cub — but when there is only silence, I leave the room.

Two or three times a year I would visit my father's office in New York City. It was on Madison Avenue near St. Patrick's Cathedral, a location my father appreciated because he could sprint, if necessary, to Grand Central when he took the train; an address my mother approved of because it was centrally located for her *day out,* as she referred to these trips. "Want to have a day out?" she would ask, and I would know it meant a visit to the city. I'd have to wear my best outfit and shoes (no sneakers), and there would be a small refresher lesson in manners, in much the same way a pilot is periodically required to get checked out on the equipment he flies.

We'd board the train at our station, and my mother would let me have the window seat so that I could gawp at the Hudson River, at the sheer rock face of the Palisades, at the expanse of the George Washington Bridge as we traveled into Manhattan. If there was a seat free, I would move to the other side of the train as we approached the city. I tried to imagine the people who lived in the tenements by the tracks. I peered down the long uptown avenues. I was awed by the tall apartment buildings and wondered, as we clicked along, if anyone actually used the balconies twenty-five stories up. We'd enter a long tunnel and then emerge to the cavernous Grand Central Station. I'd try to keep step with my mother's clicking heels as we crossed the stone floor. She would not let go of my hand until we entered the revolving door of my father's office building.

The lobby of my father's office was decorated with models in glass cases of the buildings the company had designed. Intricate and precise, with matchstick figures and bushes no bigger than my thumbnail, they were miniature universes into which I wanted to climb. My father would walk out to the lobby and make a fuss, even though we'd just seen him at breakfast. His white shirt would billow slightly over his belt, and his long sleeves would be rolled. A tie would be snug inside his collar. In exchanges as ritualized as those of a church service, he would give my mother a kiss and tell her not to spend too much money; she would laugh and tell me to be a good girl.

As my father and I walked along a corridor of cubicles, secretaries and draftsmen rolled out into the hallway to say hello or give me a high five. I remember a woman named Penny who kept hard candies in a jar and who always invited me into her cubicle to sample a few. I especially liked Angus, my father's boss, who would set me on a high stool in front of a draftsman's table and give me a set of colored pencils that had never been opened. He'd also give me a T square and a job: I'd have to draw a house or a school or the front of a store. I worked at these tasks with dedication, and the praise was always extravagant, both from Angus and from my father. "How old are you again?" Angus would ask with what appeared to be complete earnestness. "We might have to hire you right out of junior high school."

Sometimes I'd wander into my father's office and pretend to be a secretary while he was on the phone or at his drawing table. At noon he would slide his arms into the silky lining of his jacket and we'd go to lunch. We ate at a deli where I could order cheese blintzes and a bowl of coleslaw. The desserts rotated in a glass case, and I remember the agony of trying to choose among the cherry cheesecake or the éclairs or the chocolate cream pie. My father, who normally never ate dessert, would get one for himself so that I could at least taste two. After lunch we'd go to the zoo in Central Park or to a bookstore where I was allowed to pick out a book. My father would be Rob in the office, Mr. Dillon in the deli, and a freshly minted Dad to me, sophisticated and fascinating in his white shirts and suits, his overcoat swinging open as we walked the sidewalks, his arm up, finger pointed, signaling for a taxi.

By three thirty a slight sensation of fatigue and boredom would begin to overtake me, but my mother was usually prompt at four o'clock. She'd arrive, shopping bags in tow, flushed and slightly breathless from her *day out*. I always had the sensation she'd been running. The shopping bags would be exotic: some had shiny pink and white stripes; others were black with gold lettering. My father would pretend horror at the excess, but I knew he didn't really mind. Once, when they thought I'd left the room to go to the bathroom and were standing with their backs to the door, my mother took an item out and slipped it from its tissue wrap. I saw a fold of blue silk, a swath of delicate lace. My father goosed my mother, causing her to feint away and laugh.

When it was time to leave, my father would give me a tight hug, as if we were flying to Paris and he might not see us for months, even though he'd be right behind us on the six twenty. My mother and I would have to run to the train, and she would invariably fall asleep before we'd even emerged from the tunnel. I would peek into the shopping bags, taking tops off shoeboxes and fingering wool and silk and cotton. More often than not, I would fall asleep, too, resting my head on her shoulder or collapsing entirely onto her lap.

*   *   *

At dinnertime Charlotte appears wearing the jeans and the white shirt and sweater. She hugs her arms at the threshold of the kitchen. Her eyes look tired, and her nostrils are pink.

"Hi," I say.

I am fighting with a loose potato peeler. Potatoes and salad are my jobs. My father stands over the stove, frying up three chicken breasts. He has his back to Charlotte and doesn't turn when I say her name. His hair is standing up at the crown of his head, stuck that way when he pulled off his woolen cap. For most of the afternoon, he has been shoveling, racing and losing against the snow.

After leaving Charlotte's room, I went downstairs to see what my father wanted, which was simply to make sure I wasn't in Charlotte's room. Then I went to my own room to wrap the couple of Christmas presents I had to give: a hat of blue and white stripes with a rolled edge for my father, and a pair of mittens for Jo, with whom I'd shortly go skiing. I still had to finish the beaded necklace for my grandmother. Bored, I wandered into the den, where I made a fire, feeding it with bits of wood from my father's shop. The fire made me think of marshmallows, and I found a bag half-opened in a kitchen drawer. They were left over from the summer and were as hard as cardboard. I unwound a coat hanger and toasted a dozen, making myself slightly sick and spoiling my dinner. I had a rest on the sofa, legs splayed, staring at the fire until I didn't feel sick anymore. I thought about how one tiny decision can change a life. A decision that takes only a split second to make. What if, that December afternoon ten days earlier, when my father had looked up from his workbench and said *Ready?* I'd answered *No.* That I had to go inside. That I was hungry or that I had to start my homework. If we hadn't gone on that walk, there would be no Baby Doris now. She'd have died in the snow. We'd have heard about it from Marion or Sweetser, and I imagine we'd have been kind of horrified and saddened, the way you are when a crime takes place near where you live. Maybe my father and I would have felt guilty at not having taken a walk in the woods that day. There would be no Charlotte or Detective Warren, not in our lives anyway.

"Is Nicky your real name?" Charlotte asks me now in the kitchen.

I wait for my father to answer, to say *something*, and when he doesn't, I say, "It's short for Nicole." My father still has his back to Charlotte, as if he doesn't know she's in the room. "Isn't it, Dad?" I ask pointedly.

My father says nothing.

"Can I help?" Charlotte asks.

"Probably not," I say.

"I'll set the table then," she says, looking around for a table.

"We don't do it that way," I explain quietly.

"Then . . . then I'll just sit down." Seemingly baffled by the exchange, Charlotte leaves the room.

"Why are you being this way?" I ask my father when she is gone.

"What way?" he replies, taking the chicken out of the pan with tongs.

"You know . . . rude," I say.

"How are you doing with those potatoes?"

"Fine," I say, gouging into the white flesh.

Beyond the kitchen windows the wind whistles. The snow falls steadily for a minute and then whooshes hard against the glass. I think of Warren and wonder if he made it home to his two boys. I think of Baby Doris and wonder if she was collected as planned and where she is spending her first night away from the hospital.

Charlotte and my father and I sit in the den, with trays balanced on our knees, a skill my father and I have mastered but which seems to confound Charlotte. Her chicken skids across her plate, and her salad lies in bits on her lap. She picks the lettuce leaves off with delicate fingers. My father eats with determination, his face set in a mask. He will not acknowledge Charlotte's presence beyond the absolutely necessary. I eat, torn between rapt attention for Charlotte and growing impatience with my father. Charlotte, defeated by dinner, eats little and seems the most uncomfortable of the three of us, her eyes barely rising from her plate, each swallow an effort. Color rises to and recedes from her face as if she were periodically flooded by waves of shame. I think that she will bolt from her seat. My father's rigidity silences me as well. We dine to the sounds of the wind outside, and once or twice the lights flicker, reminding us that we could lose the power at any minute. After two winters in New Hampshire, my father and I have a sizable stash of candlesticks, half-burned candles, and flashlights at the ready. I like losing the power, because my father and I move into the den with its fireplace for the duration of the storm. We sleep in sleeping bags, and our ingenuity is tested in the areas of amusing ourselves and preparing meals. These episodes are cozy and warm, and I am always a little dismayed when the power — in the form of lights you'd forgotten had been left burning — comes back on with all the charm of a police spotlight.

"We're definitely going to lose our power," I say. "Charlotte and I can sleep in here. In sleeping bags."

My father gives me a frosty look.

"I'll be fine upstairs," Charlotte says.

"No you won't," I say. "There won't be any heat. The only heat will be from the fireplace. This one here."

My father rises from his seat and carries his tray out to the kitchen. Charlotte sets down her knife and fork, clearly grateful to be done with the charade. She lays her head against the chair back and shuts her eyes. I stand and take her tray and mine and follow my father. He and I share dish duty — I one night, he the other — and I'm pretty sure it's my night. But he's already begun the chore.

"You're being horrible," I say.

"This is a fiasco," he says.

When I return to the den, Charlotte still has her eyes shut, and I think she's fallen asleep. I sit across from her in my father's chair and study her. Her eyelids are bluish, and her mouth falls open slightly. I wonder where she's been and what she's been doing over the last ten days.

I think about how my father could so easily have told Warren that Charlotte was sleeping upstairs when Warren came to visit. And that would have been that. Charlotte, in my pajamas with the pink and blue bears, would have been handcuffed in our back hallway, walked out to the Jeep, and taken away. We might never have seen her again. My father would always tell me it was for the best, and I would always know that he was wrong.

I wonder where Warren keeps his handcuffs. I wonder if he wears a gun.

I pick up a book I've been reading off and on, more off than on, a sign that I'll probably abandon it soon. I find my place and try to absorb a few sentences, but I can't concentrate. I drop the book hard onto the table.

Charlotte opens her eyes.

"Do you want to see my room?" I ask.

She sits up, slightly dazed and blinking.

"I could show you a picture of my mother," I add.

"Uh, sure," she says.

We climb the stairs and enter my room, which I tidied while Charlotte was asleep. My pajamas and the empty Ring Ding package are nowhere to be seen. Charlotte seems to relax as soon as she crosses the threshold, as if my room were more familiar territory. She stands and admires the mural, or at least pretends to, and, oddly, it doesn't seem quite as amateurish as it did earlier. I think of Steve with his fictitious phone number and wonder whom he surprised with a call.

"This is great," Charlotte says with her hands tucked into the back pockets of her jeans, a posture that accentuates the bulge of her tummy. I scan the room and see it from the fresh eyes of a stranger: the desk with its shoebox of beads and coils of rawhide; the bed with the lavender-and-white quilt I brought with me from New York; the shelves of games I no longer play; the table beside the bed with its reading lamp and radio. *To Kill a Mockingbird* is on the floor. I have to read it for school.

Charlotte perches at the edge of the bed, the only place to sit apart from the desk chair.

"Have you ever worn your hair in a French braid?" she asks.

"Not really," I say.

"I think you'd look good in a French braid. Do you want me to make you one?"

"Sure."

"Sit here with me," she says. She lifts her hands to my hair and draws it back over my ears. The delicate drift of her fingers makes me close my eyes. No one has touched me this way since my mother died.

"I'll need a brush," she says.

"It's on the sill."

I move to my desk and Charlotte stands behind me. She brushes my hair upward. The brushing, like the drift of the fingers, is soothing and maternal, and I fall into a dream state somewhere between sleep and wakefulness. For a time she works without talking.

"Are you an only child?" I ask.

"No," she says. "I have two older brothers. My parents are French Canadian, very strict, very religious. My brothers are protective."

"Do they know?"

"Oh God, no," Charlotte says. "They'd kill me. For sure, my brothers would kill . . . well, you know, my boyfriend."

Boyfriend. The word sends a charge through me, much as *accomplice* did.

"Where did you live before?" she asks, drawing my hair into sections.

"New York."

"So why did you move up here?"

"My father wanted to. He says he had to, to get away

from the memories. He says he couldn't live in our house anymore."

"Didn't you mind?"

"I was angry at first. But then, I don't know, I guess I just realized it was something he had to do. I just got used to it."

I pat the beginnings of the braid she's fashioning. Expertly executed, without a misplaced hair, it makes a perfect curve against my head. "Wow," I say.

"I didn't see a TV," Charlotte says as she draws a hank of hair on my left side.

"We don't have one," I say. "I have a radio, but my father didn't want a TV. He and my mother didn't believe in letting kids watch too much TV anyway, but after the accident, I think he was afraid all he'd see on the television would be accidents and disaster."

"When did your mother and sister die?"

"Two years ago."

"You haven't had anyone fix your hair since then, have you?"

"No," I say.

Charlotte lets go of my hair. I can see her in the small round mirror over the desk. She closes her eyes. Periodically, that night and the next day, the realization of what she's done, of what happened to her in the motel room, will blow through her.

I know precisely what that feels like. When I first

moved to New Hampshire, sudden gusts of grief would overtake me on the soccer field or in the band room. Even when I wasn't actively thinking of my mother, I'd be blindsided at odd intervals. My mind would wander to a thought of her, only to find that where I used to picture her standing in the kitchen with a cup of coffee, or driving around in her VW, or knitting in front of the TV while I watched a Disney video, there was empty space. It hurt every time, and still does, like a severed nerve exposed to air.

"Are you okay?" I ask.

"I'm fine," she says. I watch as color returns to her cheeks. "The nap helped. And the food."

"You haven't been eating?"

"Not much," she says.

"We can go down later and have hot chocolate," I say. "I practically live on hot chocolate."

I hear footsteps on the landing, and a second later, a knock on the door.

Charlotte sets the brush on the desk and stands away from me.

My father enters. He looks at me and then at Charlotte and then back at me. "What's going on?" he asks.

The evidence of what we've been doing is perfectly obvious on my head.

Charlotte steps forward and around me. She doesn't

glance back as she slips past my father and walks out of the room.

"Do I have to lock her in her room?" he asks.

"No," I say.

He shakes his head. "The storm's worse," he says.

Good, I think. My father can't make Charlotte leave, and Detective Warren can't get to the house. I wish it would snow for weeks.

"You have your flashlight?" my father asks.

"Yes."

"Batteries?"

"Yup."

"From the sound of this wind, we're going to need them."

"What about her?" I ask, tilting my head in the direction of the guest room.

"I put a flashlight on her bedside table."

"What time is it?" I ask.

"About nine thirty," he says.

"You didn't say anything about my hair." I mean it as a challenge.

"What do you call it?"

"French braids."

"They're pretty." My father looks exhausted, older than his forty-two years.

He sighs. "Go to sleep," he says.

I undress and climb into my bed. I turn off my bedside light. I finger my tight new braids and listen to the moan of the wind. From time to time I imagine I hear cars in the driveway. I listen for the sound of an engine. I think about Detective Warren. Did he believe me about the ax? I don't know. Maybe he was glad my father wasn't there: easier for him to get a look around without my father watching him.

I fall asleep to the sounds of a shovel scraping against the granite steps.

The Realtor with the scarf and the fur boots showed us three houses the March day we coasted into town. The first was a cape on Strople, not far from Remy's. A fixer-upper, Mrs. Knight explained. I was horrified by the toilet in the garage, a stained bowl in which an unidentifiable animal had perished. The kitchen had green Formica counters and brown floor tiles, and it seemed unlikely I'd ever be able to eat a meal in there. I expressed my distaste by standing beside the front door and refusing to go upstairs. I needn't have worried. The house, on one of the town's most public streets, was too exposed for my father, who was looking for a cave in which to hide himself for years.

The Realtor was nosy. Where were we from? Why were we interested in Shepherd? Did we have relatives in the area? What grade was I in? My father and I were at least united in our silence: we didn't give her a thing. Had he been able to, my father would have made up the details of a life, simply to shut her up, but his imagination, like his heart, had deserted him.

The second house we visited was called Orchard Hill Farm and stood amid twelve acres of apples. It was a simple but well-kept building with a bright lemon-yellow kitchen that smelled like apples, even in March. I went upstairs and discovered four bedrooms with white curtains at the windows and high mounds of quilts on the beds. I wanted to lie down and go to sleep and wake up in New York.

My father walked through the house as a courtesy only, because next to it was a farm stand. Although we would not sell apples or whatever products had issued from that lemon-yellow kitchen, it might take a year or two before previous customers stopped coming to the house and ringing the bell. I could not imagine my father's having to go to the door time after time and explain that no, there wouldn't be any cider this year.

"I have something else," Mrs. Knight said, "but it's a bit out of town."

Magic words to my father. "I'd like to take a look," he said.

"Quite a long drive off the main road to get to it," she

said, eyeing the Saab and the small trailer. "Might be inconvenient with your daughter in school."

"I wouldn't mind having a look," my father repeated.

"We'll take my husband's truck then," Mrs. Knight decided.

The truck bounced up the drive, skidding when the snow gave way to mud. The cottage was set in a clearing that encompassed a barn as well. I knew as soon as I saw the house that this was the one my father would pick. The cottage was big enough for the two of us and was empty, a fact I knew my father would use to his advantage: we could move in right away. More to the point, it was isolated.

I had no bargaining chips. I couldn't very well lobby for the house with the grotesque toilet, nor could I argue that we should live on a farm. Besides, if it wasn't our old house in New York, did I really care anyway?

Within the hour my father had made a full-price offer, delighting the Realtor. My father and I stayed at a motel just outside of town for the ten days it took to complete the paperwork, my father driving me in the morning to the Mobil station for milk and doughnuts and after that to school, and then we moved in.

I complained incessantly. The school bus could make it only halfway up our road, and the walk was killing me, I said. My bedroom was freezing. The kids were all retarded, and the teacher was lame. There was no outlet for the hair dryer in the upstairs bathroom, and the shower had no pressure. One night, insisting that my father sit in the den with me while I completed my homework, I badgered him to help me and then interrupted him every time he tried to explain an answer. I mauled a math paper with the metal top of a pencil (popping the erasers off with my teeth was a habit I couldn't break), tearing the paper and creating a furious scribble in the wood of the coffee table beneath it. My father stood and walked out to the barn. For a time I sat with my pencil in hand. I tried to cover over the gouges in the wood with my spit. I followed my father, preparing a defense as I went: it wasn't fair; I had no friends; the kids were dorks; the house was spooky. I opened the door to the barn and at first couldn't see a thing. My father hadn't turned on the lights. But eventually, in the moonlight through the windows, I spotted him. He stood on the other side of the cavernous room, leaning against a wall. Maybe he was simply having a cigarette, but to my eye he looked exhausted and defeated, a man who knows he has lost everything.

I shut the door as quietly as I could and walked back into the house. I sat on the sofa and completed my homework easily, which I could have done all along. I searched through the cupboards and found a tin of cocoa. I boiled water in a saucepan and made two mugs of hot chocolate. I went out to the barn, carrying the mugs, loudly calling,

"Dad," as I went. Before I reached the door, the lights went on. I walked in as though nothing had transpired in the den barely an hour before. "You want some hot chocolate?" I asked.

Together we sat on a bench and blew over our mugs. "This hits the spot," he said, the effort in his voice to sound cheerful nothing short of heroic. Neither of us made any mention of the fight we'd just had.

"It's cold in here," I said.

"I'm going to try to fix up that woodstove," he said.

"I was thinking I might like to get some posters for my room."

"There must be a store in Lebanon where you can buy posters," he said. "We can check it out this weekend."

"And the other thing I'm going to need," I say, "is a desk."

My father nodded.

"What are you going to do for a job?" I asked.

"I don't know," he said, "maybe something with my hands."

I wake to a hush. The wind has stopped; there's no pinging against the windows, no whooshing against the glass. The world is completely still, as if resting after its long battle the night before. I hop on bare feet to the window because the floor is cold. The sky is gray, and snow still falls.

I put on my slippers and my bathrobe and open my bedroom door. From the kitchen I can hear the sound of the refrigerator closing. Dad must be up, I think.

But it is not my father I find in the kitchen that morning. Charlotte stands at the stove, spatula in hand. She has on the flannel pj's with the pink and blue bears and her gray angora socks. I study the cables, and for a moment all I can see is the motel room with its bloodied sheets. I look up at Charlotte's face.

"I'm making French toast," she says. Her hair is wet and waved in single ringlets down the back of her neck. Her face is scrubbed and shines clean in the overhead light. "Do you drink coffee?"

"No," I say. The change in Charlotte is unsettling. She seems rested, but it's more than that. She's somehow healthier, more robust.

Three plates and silverware have been placed on the counter near the stove. Charlotte covers one of the plates with two pieces of the toast. "I don't know if you like syrup or not," she says, "so I'll let you do it for yourself."

"You seem a lot better," I say.

The golden-tinged toast swims in melted butter. I pour a glass of juice and take my tray to the den. After a couple of minutes Charlotte follows me.

She sits on the sofa and I in my chair, as if we had already established our familial positions. Her tray tilts for a second and the syrup drips onto the flannel of the pj's. "Sorry," she says, licking it off with her finger.

She holds her hair back with one hand as she bends over her plate. She cuts her toast with her fork in a frantic motion, scraping the plate. She has the slovenly ease of someone who's eaten breakfast in the den with me for years.

"How many inches do you think we got?" she asks.

I glance out the window. "I don't know," I say. "Maybe three feet?"

"Good for the skiers," she says.

"I'm going skiing after Christmas," I say.

"Where?"

"Gunstock."

"You'll get to paint another mountain," she says.

"I already bought the paint."

Charlotte sits back, the tray still balanced on her knees. I look at my breakfast, hardly touched. My appetite has deserted me. I'm not used to this creature who can be heartbroken one minute and bursting with life the next.

"How long will it take to get plowed out?" she asks.

"I'm not sure," I say. "We're just about the last road the town gets to. It could take a day, maybe more."

"That long," she says, gazing out the window.

I don't know whether this is good news or bad. I am curious about where Charlotte will go when she leaves us.

Without explanation, I stand and take my tray to the kitchen. I feel nervous in the room with Charlotte, worried that my father will come down and find Charlotte so at ease in our house. I climb the stairs and pause at my father's door. I put my ear to the wood and can hear nothing. "Dad?" I call softly.

"Come in," he says from the other side.

He is sitting fully dressed at the edge of the bed. He has on jeans and a navy sweater over a flannel shirt. He's been pulling on his socks. His hair is matted at the sides and peaked at the top, like a screwy-looking bird in a Saturday-morning cartoon.

In the dim light I can see his bureau, covered with magazines, loose change, a balled handkerchief, a lone leather glove, and his wallet. In the corner is a chair that functions as a closet. It is piled high this morning with flannel shirts and jeans and a towel. On his bedside table are an alarm clock, a white mug, and a book about the Civil War. Also on the table are a candle in a candleholder and a flashlight. Just in case.

I take a step closer. "Are you okay?" I ask.

"Sure, why?"

"You didn't come down."

"I was up late last night."

My eyes adjust to the gloom, and I notice that my father has little thickets of gray hair over his ears. Is this new?

"Still snowing?" he asks.

"Yup."

My father stands, massaging his lower back. "I want to keep the path to the woodshed clear in case the power goes out."

"I'll do it," I say.

My father raises an eyebrow. I never offer to help with chores I hate. He walks to the window and snaps up the shades. Though the light is still the dull gray of a storm, it reflects off the surface of a small photograph on the bureau. I take a step into the room so that I can see the picture.

It is of Clara, just a year old. It would have been taken shortly before the accident. In the picture she has on a royal blue sweater, but someone, possibly me, has wrapped my father's navy scarf around her neck and put his ski cap over her head. An uneven fringe of bangs peeks out under the hat, and hair sticks out over her ears as well. Her eyes, unnaturally large, have taken on the color of the sweater. The light from the flash has caught her broad cheeks and nose, and they glow as if with an inner light. Her lower lip glistens pink. She seems delighted with her new getup and is smiling so that her top two teeth are showing. On her right eyebrow is a tiny red scab, the size of a pea.

It is a new photograph, which is to say an old photograph that has recently been put on the bureau. Though I seldom go into my father's bedroom, I am certain it was not there the night we found the baby.

Something inside me squeezes up tight, like a sponge that is being wrung out.

"She was beautiful," my father says behind me.

On the morning of Clara's first birthday, my father took me down to the cellar, where we fitted colored balloons to a tank and filled them with helium that made my father's voice, when he inhaled it, sound like Donald Duck. We brought the balloons upstairs, where they bounced around the various rooms and settled in clumps, depending upon the drafts. By nightfall they hovered two inches from the ceilings, and by noon the next day they had fallen onto the floors and chairs and behind the television, occasioning an impromptu lecture from my father on the nature of gases and air pressure and gravity. Before the accident my father was famous for his lectures, which he'd deliver in an earnest way, expecting earnest attention in return. Occasionally my mother would roll her eyes and say, with evident fondness, *Here we go again,* but I enjoyed them, being as I was, for the duration, the hot focus of his attention. Sometimes the lectures were about scientific or historic matters, but often they were moral in nature. I had the *You can do it* lecture a number of times, usually before a test or a game about which I was anxious. Memorably, I had the *Your reputation is priceless* lecture after I got invited to my first girl-boy party. And periodically I'd get the *Practice makes perfect* lecture when I complained about a math worksheet or a piece I was sick of playing on the clarinet. By the time I was nine, I could recite my father's lectures in my head as he gave them, but I was still enough in awe of him then that I didn't dare to be disrespectful. I have often wondered what would have happened to us had I reached the teenage years uninterrupted by catastrophe, at what point I'd have tried to convince myself that my father had nothing left to teach me.

The day before, my mother had driven me downtown to pick out a present for my sister. It was the first time I'd ever gone into stores by myself, and I was both excited and nervous. My mother recited a hundred rules and cautions and made me repeat the place and time we would meet three times. I was to buy the present with my own money, ten dollars I had taken from my piggy bank.

I started at a store my parents called the five-and-dime, even though nothing in the store could be purchased for five or ten cents. I wandered the aisles of the toy department, touching dolls and puzzles and board games. The problem with Clara, I decided, was that she couldn't actually *do* anything except put blocks together or fit plastic rings onto a cone. I left the store and went into a children's clothing store next door, where they sold smocked dresses and linen bonnets and where a single pair of socks cost six dollars. I tried the drugstore on the off chance there might be a terrific game in the baby aisle, but when that turned out to be a bust (save for a box of Good and Plenty), I went back to the five-and-dime. As I wandered the aisles, I began to develop the notion that what Clara really needed was a present she could grow into, something that would last and last, a toy that somehow I had missed along the way but that I could play with and then teach her how to use.

I was at the meeting place five minutes ahead of time, and so was my mother.

"What did you get?" she asked.

"Etch A Sketch," I said.

My mother made a birthday cake in the shape of a train. She let me decorate the separate cars in yellow and green and blue frosting, saving the red for the caboose. The train had a marshmallow smokestack and Life Saver windows and rode on licorice rails along the dining room table. By the time we were done, it looked like a toy, and neither one of us wanted to cut into it after we'd blown out Clara's single candle.

Clara had awakened that morning with an earache. She alternately shrieked or whined the entire day, fraying my mother's nerves and causing my father to sigh heavily and repeatedly before the first guest had even arrived. As for me, I thought my baby sister a poor sport, particularly as I was mildly jealous of all the wrapped presents in a corner, one of which I couldn't wait to get my hands on.

A birthday party for a one-year-old is never for the one-year-old. Clara was oblivious to both the festivity and the domestic angst. The party was for my parents and for me. I had not outgrown the need to be near the present that was being opened, to rip the paper myself in a kind of vicarious frenzy. Clara, immune to the excitement, had so exhausted herself with her fretting that she fell asleep as we sang "Happy Birthday" to her. My mother, reluctant to wake a cranky baby, said we should all carry on without her, an idea I approved of. Most of the photographs taken that day show Clara asleep, a cone-shaped hat on her head, her mouth parted, her nose running. I, in purple leggings and a My Little Pony T-shirt, look anxious and demanding, making sure I get my due. My mother, who that night admitted to having a toothache that later required a root canal, has frown lines between her brows. And in a picture taken by my mother long after all the guests had left, my father is asleep on the couch, crumpled paper wrapping like a small sea around his boat, Clara prone on his chest. In the photograph you can hear him snoring.

*   *   *

I am true to my word. While my father is on the telephone to my grandmother, sorting out her travel arrangements to Lebanon (all her flights have been delayed or canceled), I bundle up in my parka, snow pants, hat, and ski gloves and set out to clear the path to the woodshed for my father. My grandmother's trip will be a heroic one for a seventy-three-year-old woman, requiring driving herself to the Indianapolis airport, taking a flight from there to Newark, boarding another flight to Boston, waiting for a third flight to Lebanon on a ten-seater plane most twenty-year-olds wouldn't get on, and then being driven in my father's truck to Shepherd. Typically the trip will take her, door-to-door, eight hours. She swears that it's worth it, but I have an idea that soon she won't be able to make the journey, and that we'll have to go to Indianapolis instead, a prospect I am looking forward to. To my twelve-year-old eyes, the prospect of three plane flights in one day seems like heaven.

The snow has turned to swirls of fine icy crystals that sting my face if I don't keep my head lowered. The snow has covered the grasses and the small brush; it spreads in all directions with only the trees to break the panorama. Every pine bough and birch limb is covered with white, as is the woodshed that is my goal. Bushes make humpy shapes, and the forest has lost the spindly scratchiness of early winter. We are socked in. I think of the people who lived in the house when it was built in the late nineteenth century, when there was no town plow to make driveways and roads passable. And of the natives who lived on the land before there were any houses at all, who literally had to dig themselves up through the snow just to reach the air.

The sky seems to be clearing, and I guess that the thin snow shower is a sign of the end of the nor'easter. When the sun comes out, this same landscape will be blinding. Paralleling the drive up to the house is an open field that is long enough to make a sledding hill. Only when we've had a good snowfall, though, can I get a decent run without being slowed down by the tops of the brush. Sometimes I can talk my dad into getting out the round aluminum saucers we use for sleds and helping me pack the snow with a couple of runs himself.

I discover, as I make a few test digs, that the snow is heavy. The temperature is rising and the snow is packing itself. It could take over an hour just to reach the wood-shed, and I am beginning to regret my generosity. I hope that when my father gets off the phone with the airlines, he'll take pity and give me a hand.

I start shoveling in earnest and begin to sweat almost immediately. It takes a tremendous effort to lift a shovelful of snow high enough to overturn it. I shed the scarf and the hat and unzip my parka. After a few minutes I become predictably cold and have to put the clothes back on. I go through three cycles of dressing and undressing and have just about decided I should go in for a cup of hot chocolate when the back door opens.

"Hey," I hear a voice say.

Charlotte is half in and half out of the door. Her hair, drying, spreads across her shoulders.

"Do you have a hat and mittens I could borrow?" she asks.

"Why?"

"I want to help you shovel."

I shake my head. "You can't. You're . . ." I struggle for the word. *Sick* isn't correct. "You're, you know . . . tired," I say.

"I'm fine. I need the fresh air."

My father will be angry if he sees Charlotte outside shoveling the snow with me. Where is he, anyway? "The bench seat flips up," I say. "We have mittens and hats in there."

She slips back into the house and emerges a minute later. She takes three long breaths of air, as if she's been cooped up for days. Maybe she has. She has her jeans tucked into the tops of her boots, which are leather and not at all appropriate for the snow. She has grabbed a pair

of old leather gloves my father uses for cross-country skiing and a multicolored hat I made for myself when I was
ten. It has mistakes in it and is unraveling at the top.

"Okay," I say. "You start where I left off. I'll get the
other shovel and begin at the woodshed, and we'll meet in
the center."

The snow has drifted against the barn and rises almost
to my waist. I find the latch and lean against the door and
take a fair amount of snow into the darkened barn with
me. As always, the cavernous room smells sweetly of sawdust and pine. I don't bother to turn on the lights; I know
where the shovels are kept. My father might be sloppy in
his bedroom, but he is particular in the barn. Each of his
tools has its own place on the bench or on the Peg-Board
over it. Larger tools, such as shovels and rakes, are lined up
against the wall near the door.

Shovel hoisted, I drag my legs through the drifts. I
round the corner and see Charlotte's arms pumping, the
snow spraying to one side. She works with the strength of
a man, and I can see that she's made more progress in the
short time I've been gone than I made the whole time I
was shoveling.

She tosses off the hat, and her hair swings rhythmically
from side to side. She is breathing hard but not gasping.

Challenged, I bend to my task and try to match her
speed, but my arms simply aren't strong enough. I have

determination, but when I check out Charlotte's progress, I can see that she's making more headway than I am.

We meet closer to my end than hers. Charlotte takes the last swipe. She bangs the shovel hard against the ground to shake off the rest of the snow. "There," she says with satisfaction.

"It wasn't a race," I say.

"Who was racing?" She draws off her gloves. The snow has all but stopped.

"I'm going in," I say.

"I'll be right with you."

Inside, I sit on the bench and kick off my boots. I slip the suspenders of my snow pants off and stand in my long underwear and sweater. My hair is matted to my head and my nose is running. My mouth is so cold I can't make it work right.

"What's she doing?" my father says behind me.

I didn't hear him come down the stairs. "She was helping me shovel a little bit."

"She's shoveling?"

"Mostly she just stood there. I think she wanted some fresh air. I was about to make us some hot chocolate."

My father examines my face.

"To warm us up," I add quickly.

My father walks into the kitchen, and I think he means to pour himself a cup of coffee. Instead he stops at the counter. He puts his hands on the lip of the Formica and bends his head. Is it just coincidence that he's hovering over the telephone? Is he thinking about calling Detective Warren or Chief Boyd? He stands up and rubs the back of his neck. "I'll be in the barn," he says.

I make the hot chocolate, but still Charlotte hasn't come inside. I set the mugs on the bench in the back hallway and poke my head out the door. She has walked, or crawled, some forty feet beyond the house and stands looking into the woods. Her leather boots will be ruined.

I call her name, but either she doesn't hear me or she's so absorbed in the view that she can't acknowledge me. She has her hands in the pockets of her parka and gazes as if out to sea, as if waiting for a husband to return from a long voyage, as if searching for a child who has just wandered out of sight.

"Charlotte!" I call, my voice louder, more insistent.

She turns her head.

"Come in!" I yell.

For a moment I think she'll ignore me. Then, as I watch, she twists her body in my direction and begins to retrace her steps, aiming each foot into a boot track, much as I saw Detective Warren do just days earlier. She stumbles once, picks herself up, makes some progress, then begins to hop through the snow like a child does through the surf at the beach. She is winded when she reaches the back door.

"I made hot chocolate," I say. "Your mug's on the bench."

"Thanks," she says as she slips past me through the door.

"You weren't even looking in the right direction," I say to her back.

She sits on the bench; I'm on the stairs. I can hear her, but I can see only her boots. I want to tell her to take them off — her feet will warm up faster that way — but I hold my tongue. I imagine her cupping the mug, warming her hands, her nose and cheeks red from the cold. I can hear her blowing over the hot chocolate and then taking a sip. "Will you show me the place?" she asks.

"No."

"Why not?"

"You know why not."

"I can't see the harm in it."

"There's plenty harm in it," I say, though if pressed I'm not sure I could explain precisely what the harm might be.

"I just want to see," she says.

"Why? What possible good will that do?"

"I can't explain it."

"Don't be stupid," I say.

She is silent. I set down my mug. I put my head in my hands. "The hike would be wicked," I say after a time. "And dangerous. You've probably never even used snowshoes."

I hear her blowing her nose. "I certainly have," she says.

She has? I know so little about her life. "I'm not sure I can even find it," I say. "The snow has probably covered all the tracks."

Actually I am pretty sure I *could* find the spot. I've done the trip, back and forth, twice now and am confident I could recognize the configuration of the trees in tandem with the slope. I certainly know in which direction to head.

"The snow's stopping now," she says.

"So?"

"It'll be easy to retrace our steps. We'll make plenty of tracks."

"There's nothing there, Charlotte. Just some orange tape."

Again she says nothing, and in the extended silence I make a proposition I know is wrong, that I'll almost certainly regret. But recklessness is alive in me and pushing to get out. "All right," I say. "I'll make a deal."

"What deal?"

"You answer my questions, and maybe I'll take you," I say, knowing I'm on treacherous ground. If I ask a question and she answers it, I'll have to fulfill my part of the bargain.

"Okay," she says.

I let out my breath in a rush. "Who is he?" I ask.

"His name is James," Charlotte says without hesitation.

James, I think. "How did you meet him?" I ask.

"At college," she says. "How many questions are you going to ask me?"

"I don't know. A few. Which college?"

There's a pause. "I can't do that one," she says. "Ask me something else."

"Do you love him still?" I ask, certain she can hear the quaver in my voice.

She hesitates. "I don't know," she says carefully. "I did love him very much." She pauses. "I was crazy about him."

There is something in her voice that reminds me of the way people talk about someone who has died. Or someone loved a long time ago; still loved, perhaps, in secret.

"Does he know where you are?" I ask.

"No."

I'm relieved at this answer. I didn't like the idea of his waiting for her, out of sight, at the B&B in town perhaps.

"He was gorgeous," she adds quietly.

I have never heard a man or a boy described as gorgeous. "What does he look like?" I ask.

"He has very black curly hair that falls over his forehead. He pushes it back a lot — it's this thing that he does. And green eyes. His teeth are capped in the front from playing hockey. He's not real tall."

"Who took the baby out into the snow?" I ask, letting out a long breath.

It seems to me then, sitting on the stairs, that my future hangs upon her answer, that everything I will ever know or think about people forever depends upon what she says.

Charlotte is silent a long time. I poke my head around the corner. She is sitting with her back to the wall, staring straight out the window.

"We both agreed to go to the motel," she says carefully.

It's not the answer I wanted, but I am silent. I have asked my questions, and she has answered them. I stand, my legs weak. I press my hands against my thighs to steady them. I take another long breath and let it out.

"All right," I say. "I'll take you now."

The evening Clara was born, my father appeared at my bedroom door to tell me I'd be spending the night at Tara's. I'd been vaguely aware of small disruptions within the household — commotions of the magnitude of lost keys, say, or of a pet having an accident on the rug — minor calamities with which I didn't want to become involved. Clara, as it happened, was three weeks early, and the sudden labor pains caught my parents by surprise.

I was reading on my bed. My father seemed frantic in the way that parents do when they don't want to alarm a child but can't help themselves. He pulled clothes from bureau drawers and stuffed them into a paper bag. I went in my pajamas, my jacket wrapped around me. I said good-bye to my mother, but she had left us already, focused intently on the earthquake inside her. I wanted a hug or a kiss, and I might have gotten one had I persisted, but my father, anxious to complete his errand and return to his wife, tugged at my sleeve.

Normally a relaxed driver, my father gripped the wheel. He answered my questions with the clipped sentences of someone whose attention is elsewhere. It was only a mile from my house to Tara's, but the ride seemed to take forever. "What's wrong?" I asked. "Is Mom going to die?"

"No. Everything's fine. Just fine."

When we arrived at Tara's, Mrs. Rice's exaggerated welcome worried me even more. "If there's anything we can do . . . ," she cooed to my father's rapidly retreating back. I stood at the window and watched my father jog to his Saab. He peeled away from the curb like a teenager on a tear. *Was the baby going to die?* Tara stood beside me as I whimpered, and she bit her fingernails to the quick. "Now, now," Mrs. Rice said before suggesting the American cure for all potential disasters. "Do you want something to eat?"

Within the hour I'd forgotten my distress. Tara and I stayed up late playing Dungeons and Dragons with her brother and then slept until ten the next morning, Thanksgiving Day. So I was surprised to hear, when I entered the kitchen, that I had a new baby sister and that her name was Clara.

Later I would learn the details. My sister, clamoring to get out, was born on the elevator, much to the horror of the hospital attendant who was accompanying my mother in her wheelchair up to Labor and Delivery. The attendant stopped the elevator at the first available floor, shouted for help, and my sister was technically delivered by an orthopedist in shirt and tie who was waiting to go home to his family after a long shift at the hospital. Everyone was frazzled, most of all my father, who had dropped to his knees to catch his daughter before she hit the floor.

My father came to fetch me to take me to the hospital. He was a different father than the one who had left me at the Rices' the night before. He whistled as he drove with one finger on the wheel, and he related the story about the elevator, all the while chuckling to himself as if he'd just been told a terrific joke. He took me up to the nursery and pointed out my sister. I thought he'd made a mistake. I checked the name. No mistake. The small label above the cot read *Baby Baker-Dillon.*

Clara's head was misshapen and her eyes were ratlike slits. Her skin was a mottled red and purple when she cried. She didn't look at all like the babies in the magazines, and when my father said to me, "Isn't she beautiful?" I was speechless.

I was taken to visit my mother, who was loopy and bloated. She echoed my father — "Did you see her? Isn't she beautiful?" — which I found deeply upsetting. What was wrong with my parents? Didn't they see the same things I did? "We have a Thanksgiving baby," my mother crowed.

I was returned to the Rices, where I was to have my Thanksgiving dinner. Few events in a child's life are as subtly unsettling as a holiday dinner with a family not one's own. The food was all wrong — the Rices served peas and Jell-O salad and scalloped oysters, which I mistook for stuffing and had to spit out — and the kids' table was in the kitchen, my head level with congealing gravy in a pan on a counter. Throughout dinner, I would suddenly remember — like a leftover wisp of nightmare — that I had an ugly baby sister, a truth that rattled me and made me furtive.

My mother and the baby went home the next morning, and once again my father came to fetch me. I collected my clothes in the wrinkled paper bag and followed him to the car. He was white-faced, ashen from exhaustion, and he didn't whistle. Feeling gypped and betrayed, I asked no questions and stared out my window. *I don't have to like this,* I kept reminding myself.

Once inside the house, my father tossed his keys on the kitchen counter. I set down my paper bag and let my jacket slip to the floor. I could hear my mother calling my name from her bedroom.

"Go ahead," my father said, sensing my reluctance.

Slowly I climbed the stairs. I hesitated at the bedroom door. My mother looked soft and lumpy in a silk kimono my father had given her. Her hair was pulled back in a ponytail, and she had short red socks on. "Come in," she said, waving me toward her. "Come sit with us on the bed."

I climbed onto the high white bed and knelt in front of my mother. She was holding Clara, who was sleeping. Already my sister had lost the mottled coloring of a day earlier. She made tiny kissing motions with her mouth, a delicate and pouty bow. "You want to hold her?" my mother asked.

I did not want to hold her, just as I would not, years later, want to sit behind the wheel of a car for the first time or traverse a glacier, clipped to a guide wire. I was afraid; I didn't know what to do. I thought that I might smother Clara or break her. At the very least I'd make a fool of myself. But my mother persisted, gently encouraging me. "Go on," she whispered, as if my holding the baby were a secret just between us. "You can do it."

I turned and braced my back against the headboard. My mother slid the baby carefully into my arms. Clara was wrapped like a papoose, and I was instantly amazed by her weight and her warmth. She didn't look like a rat anymore, more like a pig. She opened one eye, looked me straight in the face, and then closed it. I laughed. I was sure that she was saying, *Hey Sis — catch you later when I can see and talk.*

My father stepped into the room. He held the camera

up and took a picture. For all the time that we lived in New York, the framed photograph sat atop the mantelpiece in the living room. When we moved to New Hampshire, I insisted that my father unpack it and put it on a shelf in the den. In the photograph I look giddy, as if I'd just been tickled from inside with a feather.

I dress as if preparing for a mission in Alaska. I lend Charlotte mittens and a scarf and a better hat, all the while expecting my father to appear, bark at us, and send me to my room. There isn't much I can do about Charlotte's leather boots. She wears a size nine; I am a size six and a half; my father wears a twelve. "I'll be fine," she says. "I don't care about the boots."

Once outside I give her a crash course in snowshoeing. "There's not much to it," I say. "You strap them on and start walking. Like this," I add, demonstrating.

"I know how to do this," she says.

Charlotte climbs up onto the snowbank and moves as if her legs are blocks of wood she needs to haul around. I tell her to relax, all the while casting quick glances toward the barn. I think I hear the sound of a saw, or at least I hope I do. We might make it to the edge of the woods without his noticing us. I can't ever remember a time when I've had to sneak away from my house; for the last two and a half years, there hasn't been anywhere to go.

Charlotte is panting by the time we reach a spot where we can stop to catch our breath. She bends over and puts her hands on her knees, a runner after a marathon. I ask her half a dozen times if she's okay, and finally she tells me to quit it, she is fine. I know that if my father catches us (actually, I already know that it's *when*, not *if*), my most flagrant transgression will not be having taken Charlotte to see the place where her baby was left to die, but rather that I risked her life in getting her there. I am trusting in Charlotte, a person I hardly know, to warn me if she's in serious trouble.

"You're sure you can do this?" I ask.

"I'm positive."

The snow, dislodged from pine boughs above, falls in delicate showers. Charlotte begins to sweat. She unwinds the scarf and unzips her jacket to her stomach. Her jeans are wet to her knees, and I don't want to think about her leather boots. I feel each footfall as a step toward disaster, but pride or inevitability or simply forward momentum keeps me going.

After a time I stop thinking about disaster and my father and Charlotte and begin to concentrate on navigating. I can see the path clearly in my mind's eye; finding it from the forest floor is another matter. I recognize a rocky outcropping and locate the place where my father and I veered right, but after that I move more by instinct than by certain knowledge. Were we climbing as we moved sideways around the mountain to the right? I try to remember and wish I'd paid more attention during our second hike to the spot the day we ran into Detective Warren.

Charlotte and I fall into a routine. I walk a hundred feet, turn to see that she's behind me, and wait for her to catch up. She doesn't look quite as ungainly as she did when we set out, and she's making better progress. As I wait for her, visions of catastrophe begin to crowd the edges of my thoughts, but I push them away. Jeopardizing Charlotte's health will not be the worst crime my father will accuse me of, I now realize. The worst crime will be getting lost and forcing others to come find us. *If* they can find us.

We walk until we come to a clearing I have never seen before. I try to convince myself that my father and I simply bypassed it during our earlier treks, but I know that isn't so. I hate telling Charlotte I've taken a wrong turn almost as much as admitting it to myself, but I have no choice.

Charlotte, too winded, says nothing.

"We'll find it," I say.

We retrace our steps, easy to follow in the pristine snow. Tiny V's of bird tracks make faint impressions on the surface, and occasionally I can see the small scuff marks of an animal on the run. The challenge, I know, is to find the place where I went wrong. I walk slowly, like a hunter, examining every tree, every lower branch for some sign of breakage, but the bushes my father and I might have disturbed are mostly covered with snow. It is as if Charlotte and I are floating atop the forest floor.

I've already admitted defeat to myself, if not to Charlotte, when I see, in the distance, the tiniest blot of raspberry. "Wait here," I say.

I move as quickly as I'm able. When I come within thirty feet of the reddish color, I see that it's the item I hoped it was: my hat, the one I lost on the first night. It's caught within a tangle of brush, possibly blown there by the winds of the night before. It might not mark the trail precisely, but I know that the path can't be too far away. I yell for Charlotte to join me.

I reach for my hat in the brush. I'm glad to have it back. I hate losing anything I've knit.

"My hat," I say to Charlotte when she reaches me. "The path has to be near here."

The trail my father and I made, twice coming and going, has created a faint depression, as if a brook were running beneath the snow. I motion to Charlotte to follow me. I keep to the muffled trail. We hike for another fifteen minutes until I see, in the distance, a telltale sliver of orange tape.

I wait for Charlotte to catch up. "That's it," I say, pointing.

Charlotte stands a minute, trying to slow her breathing.

I wait to see what she will do. My job is done. I am simply the guide. I have no place here except to show her the way home.

Charlotte moves forward and I follow, our positions now reversed. A wind bends the tops of the pines, sending snow dust to the ground.

Charlotte slips under the orange tape.

The footprints with their outlines of red paint have been erased. The mound of snow might be a bed for a burrowing animal. I refuse to think about how a baby might have lain here covered, as if with a heaping pile of quilts.

Charlotte walks to the center and kneels. She has on the purple-and-white-striped hat I gave her; she's taken off the mittens already. Kneeling in the snow in snowshoes is always awkward at best. They bend her feet and dig in at the small of her back.

She scoops up snow and brings it to her face. She covers her mouth and nose and eyes. She holds it there for what seems like minutes. It begins to melt from the warmth of her face and dribbles off her chin. She is crying, her shoulders shaking. She makes a quick feline movement and lies over the snow, her face buried.

I stand outside the enclosure. When she has not moved in some time, I say her name. "Charlotte?"

She snaps back up onto her knees and begins to cuff the snow. First with her right hand and then with her left. Right, left. Right, left. Right, left. Angry swipes accompanied by words I can't at first make out. I think she's simply groaning or crying, but then I hear the word *stupid*. And after that, the words *could I*. She bends forward and slaps at the snow in a frenzy. I hear her say, *God, God, God*.

I did not imagine this. I pictured a quiet scene, satisfying and healing. Not this fury. Not this hurtling grief.

Charlotte turns and sits on the snow, her legs to one side, her hands braced behind her. Her face is crimson and wet.

I wait, feeling as helpless as I ever have.

"God," she says. Not to me, and not to any god she might or might not believe in. She lifts her face to the sky.

She leans forward and crosses her arms over her chest. She bends her head, as if closing in on herself. She remains that way for five, maybe ten minutes, without moving.

"Charlotte?" I ask.

She glances up and seems surprised to see me there. She pushes her hair off her face.

"I think we'd better go back," I say.

With difficulty, she stands. She stumbles on the snowshoes. She leaves the enclosure, slipping under the tape. I see that she has left the purple-and-white hat behind, but I don't want to ask her to go back for it.

"You walk in front this time," I say. "The tracks will be easy to follow. I'll let you know if you go wrong."

Her face is scratched and chapped. The bruise on her chin from when she hit the corner of the table is turning yellow and green. She looks as though she's been beaten up. I slip back to get the hat and stuff it into my pocket. I watch the back of her blue parka as I follow her. She wipes her nose on her sleeve, which can't be much help. I think about her scratched face and worry that she might have given herself frostbite when she put her face in the snow.

Charlotte moves slowly, and it's hard not to step on her snowshoes. I don't want to lead, however, because I'm afraid she might simply lie down or wander off. I wonder at her rage and grief. Was it rage at herself or at the man who left the baby there? Not a man, a boy. A college boy. A student, like herself. She is only nineteen. Is a nineteen-year-old a girl or a woman? I wonder. A boy or a man?

At the place where I took the wrong turn, I call ahead to her and tell her which is the correct path. She's an automaton on bamboo, proceeding forward because there isn't any other alternative. If she stops she'll lie down and curl up in the snow, and I'll never get her to stand up. She stumbles once and puts her hands out to stop her fall. She scrapes her palms on the rough bark of a pine tree.

"Put your mittens on," I say.

After we pass the halfway point, I realize that I'm hungry. I haven't had anything to eat since breakfast, and I hardly ate that. I fish in my pockets for a piece of gum or a crumpled cracker in cellophane, left over from a school lunch. Charlotte stops in front of me, and I tread on the backs of her snowshoes.

"What?" I ask.

When she says nothing, I peer around her. In the distance I can see a moving beige shape.

"Crap," I say.

I walk forward to meet my father, because I know he'll be even angrier if he's forced to make his way to us. We meet on the path in our snowshoes. His fury is tight and monumental.

"What in God's name are you up to?" he asks through his nearly frozen mouth.

"I was just —"

"Do you have any idea what you've done?" he asks, interrupting me. "She might have fainted again. You might have gotten lost. You both might have died."

I hardly recognize my father's contorted face. He points in the direction from which he came. "I want you in that house just as fast as your legs can get you there," he says. He looks around me at Charlotte. "And as for you . . . ," he begins.

But the ruin of Charlotte's face silences him. The scratches are more prominent now, and her eyes are swollen.

"What happened?" he asks.

Neither Charlotte nor I answer him. I can't think how I'd even begin to describe what took place within the orange circle. I know, as one does at twelve or eleven or ten, that I have witnessed something I shouldn't have witnessed, seen something I shouldn't have seen. I know already that I will not be able to erase the image of Charlotte cuffing the snow in a frenzy.

I walk through the trees, knowing that my father will have to wait for Charlotte. I don't want to be told to go to my room. I'll go there of my own accord and climb into bed and pull the covers over my head. With any luck I'll fall asleep and wake up with no memory of the last hour.

The path is easy to follow: three people in their snow-shoes have trampled it. My father, in his anger, has made the deepest cuts of all. Snow begins to fall before I reach the house.

I've always been amazed by the onset of a snowfall. First a few tiny flakes dot the air, so that I'm not sure if it's actually snowing or the wind is blowing it off the tree branches. Then there is a gentle and pervasive fall that resembles the snow of movies or of Christmas cards.

Before I've walked fifteen minutes away from Charlotte and my father, I feel as though I'm caught in a blizzard. I think of waiting on the path in case the snow covers the tracks before my father and Charlotte reach the point where I'm standing, but then I reason that my father will surely know the way. I don't want to think of their silent trek, Charlotte walking ahead, my father taking up the rear, two strangers in the woods.

At the house I unbuckle my snowshoes, go inside, find a package of Ring Dings in a cupboard in the kitchen, and hurry up to my room. I let my wet and soggy clothes slide to the floor until I have on only my underwear. Looking into the mirror over the desk, I see that my face is chapped red and my hair is stringy. I walk to the bed, sit at its edge, and stuff the Ring Dings into my mouth.

Still chewing, I lie down and pull the covers up to my chin. The world beyond my window is opaque. I hear a door open and close and the stomping of boots against the mat in the back hallway. The door opens and closes a second time, another stomping of boots. There's no exchange of words, merely a stocking-footed tread on the stairs. I hear the creak of the guest room door, then a second tread on the stairs, this one heavier than the first. My father's bedroom door swishes closed. I lie in my bed and listen, but there is only silence.

I awake to a knock on the door. It seems colder in my bedroom than it ought to be. I prop myself up on my elbows. I notice that it's dark outside.

"Nicky," my father says.

"Just a minute."

I toss the covers aside, snatch my bathrobe from the back of the door, and put it on. I tie the sash and open the door.

My father stands in a darkened hallway. He has a flashlight pointed toward the floor, and I can just make out his face.

"We've lost the power," he says.

"What time is it?"

"Seven. Get dressed and come down to the den. And wake her up and get her down, too." My father still won't say her name. "And Nicky."

"What?"

"Don't you *ever* . . . and I mean *ever* . . . pull a stunt like that again."

I concentrate on the spot of light on the floor.

"Another half hour and I wouldn't have been able to find you," he says. The fury is gone from his voice, but the parental scold is not.

"I'm sorry," I say.

"I should hope so," my father says in the dark.

I have to shake Charlotte's shoulder to wake her. She sleeps with her face smashed against the pillow, her mouth slightly parted. I wonder, just before I touch her, what she dreams of. Of her boyfriend, whose name is James? Of Baby Doris before she was Baby Doris? Or are her dreams more specific and more terrifying — of a baby hidden beneath a mound of snow?

"The power's out," I tell her when she sits up. "We have to go down to the den. There's a fireplace there."

She seems disoriented. "What?" she asks.

"Dress warm," I say.

"What time is it?"

"Seven. You've got a flashlight here on this table. Use it. Especially on the stairs."

There's a fire in the fireplace when I arrive in the den. A half-dozen candles have been lit and set on a side table and the coffee table. I know from prior experience to over-dress. I have on two sweaters, long underwear under my jeans, and two pairs of socks. I can hear my father in the kitchen. I go to the window and peer out at the snow. The storm has stopped, and the cloud cover is breaking up. To the west are stars and the moon. I love the look of moon-light on the snow, the liquid blue of a molded landscape. Beside the sofa are two rolled sleeping bags. Normally these would be for my father and me, who would sleep close to the fire during the night, but I guess that now they will be for me and Charlotte. My father, I know, will not sleep in the same room as Charlotte.

My father enters the den. "She's coming down?" he asks.

"Yup."

"That sweater there, that's for her." A heavy gray sweater has been folded and set atop the armrest of the sofa.

"What are you making?" I ask.

"Scrambled eggs and bacon."

My father will be able to stay warm in the kitchen by lighting the gas stove. That's probably where he'll sleep, I now realize.

I kneel in front of the fire, feeding it bits of kindling. There are two scorch marks in the wood floor where sparks landed when a log toppled. The inside of the fire-place is black with chimney soot.

Charlotte appears in the doorway. She has her pink sweater pulled tight across her chest. Her hair is freshly brushed, and her skin is rosy in the firelight.

"My dad's making dinner," I say. "Are you hungry?"

"Yes."

"Me, too. I'm starving."

Charlotte sits on the sofa with her arms crossed in front of her.

"What happened on the walk back?" I ask. "Did my dad say anything?"

"No," she says.

"Not a word?"

"Nothing."

"Wow," I say, my generic response to all statements. My hand brushes the hem of her jeans. "They're wet," I say.

"Just damp."

"You'll freeze."

"I'm all right."

"Wait here."

I climb the stairs to my father's room. I search for a pile of clean laundry, distinguished from the dirty laundry on the floor only by the fact that the clean clothes are folded. My father's pants will swim on Charlotte.

"I can't," Charlotte says when she sees what I've brought her.

"You can," I say evenly. I'm not my father's daughter for nothing. "Put these on. There's a belt here. And that sweater there is for you. It'll be warmer than your sweater."

Charlotte hesitates, then stands. She takes the clothes and walks toward the front room.

"Hang your jeans to dry," I call, "on a door or something."

I set the trays and pour the milk, opening and shutting the fridge as if a wild animal were inside and wanted to escape. My father serves up the scrambled eggs. I'm salivating from the pungent smell of the bacon.

I balance two trays in my hands and find Charlotte sitting on the sofa in what is rapidly becoming her spot. She has rolled the cuffs of the jeans and has my father's sweater on over her own pink sweater. She looks as though she were playing him at a Halloween party. I set a tray in front of her. She examines it but makes no move to pick up a fork.

My father enters with his tray and the lantern, clearly taken aback to see Charlotte in his clothes. In the lantern light, the windows are black and reflective. I can see my face, distorted, in the old glass.

Charlotte lifts her fork and takes a restrained bite. I know she must be as hungry as I am, but her gestures are stiff and formal. I'm less restrained, and were it not for the power outage or my father's painfully rigid silence, he almost certainly would tell me not to shovel my food.

What makes a family? I wonder. My father and I are technically a family, but it's a word neither one of us would ever use. Yes, we are father and daughter, but because we were once members of a family that was torn apart, we think of ourselves now as half a family or a shadow family. As we sit there with our trays on our laps, however, I feel, or perhaps only imagine, a "family" consisting of my father, Charlotte, and me.

I imagine it because I want it. I want an older sister who will not be a replacement for my mother or Clara, but instead something in between. Someone who will tell me how to wear my hair or what to say to a boy, who might know how to dress. My father, Charlotte, and I do not have blood in common, but we are united by a person whose presence hovers in that room, who might be lying in the center of that room on warm, soft cushions.

"This is good," Charlotte says.

My father shrugs.

The telephone rings, a harsh and foreign sound. I always forget that when the power is out, the telephone still works. For a moment none of us moves. I think about Detective Warren. I jump up. "I'll get it," I say.

I'm relieved when I hear Jo's voice at the other end. "Hi," I say.

"What are you doing?" Jo asks.

"Eating."

"I'm so bored."

I glance over into the den. Jo wouldn't be so bored if she knew that the mother of the abandoned baby was sitting across from my father.

"This storm is a drag," Jo says.

"Yeah."

"We were going to the movies before this."

"With who?"

"My cousins. You're still coming skiing?"

"Yup," I say.

"So what did you do all day?"

I took the mother of the abandoned baby into the woods and watched her go nuts.

"Nothing," I say. "Wrapped a few presents."

"Me, too."

"I kind of have to go," I say. "Call me later?"

"Sure," Jo says.

I hang up the telephone. I stand a minute in the kitchen. I eat another piece of bacon. When I return to the den, Charlotte has finished her dinner and sits primly, as if waiting for instructions. My father finishes his meal.

Charlotte stands and removes my father's tray from his hands and slips it under her own. I watch her walk out to the kitchen.

"What did Jo want?" my father asks.

"Nothing," I say. "I don't know why you do that."

"Do what?" my father asks, though he knows perfectly well what I mean.

"Not talk to Charlotte. I don't get it. Is it going to kill you to talk to her?"

"I hardly know her," my father says.

"She doesn't want to *live* here," I say. "She keeps saying she wants to leave."

"And as soon as we get plowed out, she will," my father says, standing. "This isn't a social occasion."

"What would you know about social occasions?" I snap.

When I reach the kitchen, Charlotte is scraping the plates. I set the lantern on the stove. Charlotte's hair is burnished gold in the light.

"Do you play chess?" I ask.

"Not really," she says.

"You feel like toasting marshmallows?"

"In the fire?"

"Yes."

"Um, not really. But you have some," she says.

I remember how sick I felt yesterday. I can hear my father shoveling outside.

"But if you have another game or something, I'll play it with you," she adds.

"What did you used to do at night?" I ask. "When you lived with James?"

As soon as I ask the question, I'm embarrassed. Probably they had sex all night.

"He'd get home from practice late. We'd eat. We might listen to music for a while. Then he'd study. I might read or watch TV. Sometimes I'd knit."

"You knit?" I ask, surprised.

She nods.

"I knit all the time," I say, barely able to contain my excitement. "That hat you wore today? The purple-and-white one? I knit that, like, a year ago."

"Cool," she says.

"I never meet anyone who knits. Except old ladies. Marion down at the store knits."

"Who taught you?"

"My mother."

"My grandmother taught me," Charlotte says. "She taught me to knit and to paint and to sew. She used to insist that I speak only French to her."

"Not your mother?" I ask.

"My mother's always worked at the mill." Charlotte puts all the dirty dishes in the sink. She wipes off the trays and sets them onto the top of the fridge. "In the summer James and I would sit in the backyard. The landlord let me have a garden. I had some vegetables, but mostly flowers."

My father has set the stove to two hundred degrees, which is enough to warm the kitchen, but there are no chairs in the room on which to sit. I return to the den, just as my father is bringing in a load of wood. He sets it by the fire without a word and goes outside again. After a time, Charlotte joins me by the fire.

"What year are you in school?" I ask.

"Sophomore," she says.

"You won't go back?" I ask.

"No," she says. "Not there anyway."

"Because he might be there?"

"He plays hockey. He's on a scholarship for it." She pauses. "He wants to go to medical school."

"Wow," I say, picking at the rug.

"It's why I couldn't tell anyone," she says.

"Didn't anyone notice?"

"I wore loose sweatshirts and sweatpants," she says. "I had one seminar course, which I dropped. The rest were lecture courses in auditoriums. Eventually I dropped those, too."

"But didn't your friends or roommate say anything?"

"I spent all my time at James's apartment. I hardly ever saw my roommate. Maybe she thought I was putting on weight, I don't know. I gained weight all over. You probably wouldn't think it to look at me, but I'm supposed to be skinny."

I cannot imagine it. Charlotte looks perfect as she is.

"People probably would have begun to notice except that the baby came early," she says. "A month, I think."

"You don't know?" I ask.

"Not really."

"Your family didn't know about the baby?"

"My parents would have killed me. They're strict Catholics. And my brothers — I can't even think what my brothers would have done." She shakes her head once quickly. "I know this is kind of hard to understand," she says, looking straight at me. "But I kind of gave myself over to him. To James."

"You did?"

"And Nicky?"

"Yes?"

"I wanted the baby. I really wanted it."

"What's it feel like?" I ask.

She tilts her head and studies me. "You don't have anyone to talk to about this, do you?"

"No."

"You can't ask your father."

"No."

"A friend?" she asks.

I think about Jo, the Viking goddess. "I don't think she knows any more than I do," I say.

Charlotte brings her knees to her chest and wraps her arms around them. The position must hurt, though, because she immediately sets her legs to one side. "It's unlike anything you can ever imagine," she says.

The world outside our house is silent — no humming of motors, no groans from the furnace, only the fire snaps. Occasionally, through the windows, I can hear the scrape of a shovel against the snow.

"You know that something is, I won't say wrong, but different," she says. "Right away. Food doesn't taste right." She touches her throat. "There's a kind of metallic taste right here. Foods you used to like a lot smell bad. And your breasts hurt. They get swollen and tender. And then you realize you didn't get your period when you were supposed to. So I bought a test. In a drugstore? And there it was, big as life. The pink doughnut."

I am pretty sure I know what the pink doughnut means.

"I waited another couple of weeks before I told James. By then I wasn't feeling well. I was queasy, not just in the mornings, either. It's sort of a headachy, sick-to-your-stomach feeling."

"So then you told him?" I asked.

"I did," she says.

"And what did he say?"

"He was shocked at first and kept asking how this could have happened. We had always been pretty careful." She glances at me to see whether or not I know what *being careful* means. I nod, though I'm a little fuzzy on the details.

"He paced a lot," she says. "Sometimes he'd say, 'What are we going to do?' and then he'd ask me how I was. He wasn't happy about it. I think he could see his whole life draining away."

I hate James even more than I did before. "But what about your life?" I ask. "Did he care about that?"

"He cared," she says, "of course he cared. He didn't ask me to get rid of the baby. He's Catholic, too, and I think he knew enough not to ask me to do that. But he did talk about giving the baby up when it was born. He just kept saying, 'We'll take this one step at a time.'" She stops for a moment and arches her back. I have the feeling that it's hurting her. "The morning sickness goes away, and it feels . . . it just feels . . . so wonderful, I can't explain it. You feel the baby kick," she says. "It's an inside tickle, like gas bubbles moving around. But different. Everything is different from anything you've ever felt before. And you feel . . . full. Just full." She smiles. "Even though you're always hungry. I craved doughnuts most of all. Nothing on them, just the plain, but hot, with a crispy outside. I ate them with milk."

Charlotte stretches her legs in front of her and leans

back, propping herself up with her elbows. She yawns. "It'll be different for you," she says, looking at me. "It will be wonderful and perfect, and it won't have a bad ending. I'm sure of that."

Charlotte yawns again. "Thank you for taking me to the place," she says. "I'm sorry it got you in trouble with your dad."

"That's okay," I say. "He'll get over it."

I sit to one side of the fire, poking it from time to time to make the flames burn brighter. I put on another log. I remember that I still need to finish my grandmother's necklace.

I reach for the flashlight and stand. "I have to go up to my room," I tell Charlotte, "and get my beads."

Charlotte yawns again. "The fire is making me sleepy."

I could find my way without a flashlight, but I use it anyway. I locate the shoebox of beads and rawhide and bring it down to the den. I set it near the hearth so that I can distinguish the beads in the firelight. I rummage around in the box to find a crimp.

"That's beautiful," Charlotte says.

"It's for my grandmother."

The necklace has six round black Kenyan beads with a silver pendant in the center.

"I'd wear that," Charlotte says. "You must have a very cool grandmother."

Charlotte watches me fuss with the crimp, always the

hardest part of making a necklace. "I have to fit this rawhide into this little thingy here," I say, "and then clamp it down so the rawhide won't come out. This makes the catch."

"Oh," she says.

I slide the end of the fine rawhide into the crimp. I use the crimper to flatten it. When I'm done, I pull on the rawhide to make sure the crimp worked. The rawhide springs free. "Crap," I say.

I search through the beads in my box for another crimp. I might have one in my desk drawer upstairs, but I don't want to have to go all the way up there again.

The beads in the box flicker and catch the firelight. I have glass pony beads and crow beads, seed beads and Bali silver beads. "What's this one?" Charlotte asks, holding a blue glass bead up to the light.

"It's Czechoslovakian. It's a fire-polished bead."

"What does that mean?"

"I don't know."

"It's beautiful," she says.

"You should see it in the daylight. Do you want it?"

"Oh, no," she says, dropping the bead into the box.

I take it out again. "I have six of them," I say. "You could make a necklace, too."

"But they're your beads," Charlotte says.

"I have a lot of beads," I say.

Charlotte looks at me and tilts her head the way she often does. "Thanks," she says.

I hand her a coil of rawhide. I search the box for the remaining five blue glass beads. The color is hard to detect in the dark, but the beads have a distinctive shape — round and multifaceted. Charlotte sets the beads on the floor and then begins to string them.

I pick up my grandmother's necklace and hold it up to the firelight. There's a sheen on the beads and the pendant is perfectly centered.

I glance over at Charlotte. She has strung the beads on the rawhide. "Wait a sec," I say. "I should have told you. If you do it like that, the beads will slide around and the clasp will end up in the front. What you have to do is put a knot on either side of each bead. Because you have six beads, you have to put your first knot in the exact center of the string."

I reach over to show her. I make a simple overhand knot.

"Okay," she says.

I hand her the rawhide. I watch as she slides a bead on. Her delicate fingers make an easy knot, nicely placed. Her hair hangs down around her face, and she has to flip it to one side so that she can see in the firelight. I watch as she strings another bead and another and then begins on the opposite side. It's a simple necklace to make — they're all simple, really — but it's her first, and spacing the knots on the opposite side to match the first side is sometimes a little tricky.

For a while I simply observe. Charlotte's face is tight with concentration. She must look like this when she's studying, I think.

When she has strung the last bead, she holds the necklace up to the light. The facets sparkle. "Looks great," I say.

Charlotte lays the necklace against the small triangle of skin inside the collar of her white shirt and my father's V-neck sweater.

"You'll love it in the morning," I add.

Earlier, when I was rummaging through the box for the six blue beads, I felt a second crimp under my fingers. "I think I've got one in here somewhere," I say, holding the box up and tipping it toward the light. I sift through the beads. A bit of silver catches the light. "So here's the hard part," I say.

The telephone rings. Again, it seems wrong in the cozy firelight, as if something from one century had crept into another. I glance over at the kitchen. "Jo again," I say, standing. "I'll be right back."

I walk into the kitchen and pick up the phone. "Hi," I say.

"Nicky?"

I spin around, my back to the den.

"This is Detective Warren. Is your dad there?"

I hear the rhythmic scrape of the shovel outside. I take a quick breath.

"No," I say. "He's in the shower."

I can hear Charlotte behind me in the doorway.

"Tell him to call me when he gets out, okay?" Warren asks.

"Sure."

"Let me give you the number."

Detective Warren gives me a phone number, which I don't write down.

"Your power out?" he asks.

"Yes."

"Here, too. Stay warm."

"We will," I say.

I hang up the phone. I turn and look at Charlotte.

"Oh God," I say.

"What?" Charlotte asks.

"It was that detective."

Charlotte's face is expressionless. "What did he want?"

"He wanted my dad." I feel breathless with my crime. "I said he was in the shower."

"I'll go in the morning," Charlotte says. "You can't keep this up."

I think about how my father drove to the police station

in back of the post office, how he intended to tell Chief Boyd. If Chief Boyd had been there, Charlotte would be in jail now.

Charlotte turns and walks into the den. I follow her. She stands a minute by the fire. "Maybe I should go to bed," she says.

I'm not sleepy in the slightest.

She scans the room. "We're supposed to sleep here?"

I roll out the two sleeping bags. I put hers closest to the fire because that's the best spot. I think about everything Charlotte told me. How could a man really love a woman and expect her to give up her baby once it was born? The idea of giving up a baby — never mind leaving it to die — is incomprehensible to me. I can't imagine it. Wouldn't it just hurt your whole life, just like losing Clara always hurts me even if I don't think about it every second? It's why I've had to create the idea of Clara still growing, still alive. It's where I send my thoughts whenever I start to think about her.

Charlotte climbs into her bag and adjusts her pillow. I sit to one side of the fire, poking it from time to time to make the flames burn brighter. I put on another log. I'm still not sleepy.

Charlotte falls asleep at once. I listen as she begins to snore lightly.

I work on Charlotte's necklace until I've finished it. I set it in the box. In the morning I'll insist she put it on. I climb into my sleeping bag and stare at the ceiling. I think about morning sickness and the pink doughnut. I wonder about a metallic taste at the back of the throat. I glance over at Charlotte and realize once again that she is the mother of a baby that was left to die. She is sleeping in our house, on the floor, right next to me. She might get caught and go to jail. My father and I might go to jail.

I roll over and watch the fire. I might have to lie awake for hours, I decide. I might have to go find my book and read it with the flashlight.

But after a time, I begin to picture a different future — one in which Charlotte doesn't get caught; one in which she gets her baby back; one in which she and her baby live with my father and me.

I see this future in great detail. A white crib in the guest room; in the den, an old high chair with a red leather seat that I once saw at Sweetser's. A blue stroller in the back hallway; in Charlotte's car, a padded baby seat. I'll go to school during the day, and when I get home Charlotte will be pacing the back hallway with the baby on her hip. She'll have on her fuzzy pink sweater and a pair of jeans. She'll have chocolate-chip brownies waiting for me, and she'll ask me questions about my boyfriend. She'll have an errand to do, or maybe she'll go to school in the evenings, and she'll ask me to babysit. At night, while we do our homework together, we'll have to talk quietly so we won't wake the baby up. Charlotte will take me to Hanover to get my hair frosted, and she'll drive me and my friends to the movies.

There will be no James.

My father will come around.

I'll make Charlotte an ankle bracelet, and I'll knit a blanket for the baby out of the pastel multicolor yarn that Marion is always trying to palm off on me and I never take. No, I'll make it out of the soft yellow yarn I once saw at Ames in Newport. Charlotte will take me to the store, and I'll buy the yarn with my own money. I'm thinking about a basket-weave pattern when the warmth of the fire begins to work on me as it must have done on Charlotte. The last sound I hear is that of my father stomping the snow from his boots in the back hallway.

I wake once during the night — there's a disturbance — but I'm so tired from the shoveling and the hiking and the nervous atmosphere in the house since Charlotte's arrival that I go back to sleep almost immediately. I wake again, however, just a short time later, to the sound of voices from the kitchen. I don't want the voices to be there, I want to slip back into my dream, but the fact of the voices makes me open my eyes. Voices? There are murmurs, long strings of syllables, clipped answers, but I can't actually hear the words. The fire has mostly gone out, and only a few embers glow. Charlotte, I see, is not in her sleeping bag.

Later I will learn that Charlotte, waking during the night and wanting a glass of milk — and not knowing that my father would be sleeping in the kitchen — tripped over the sleeping bag (with my father in it) and smashed her palms hard into the grillwork on the stove. My father woke and examined Charlotte's hands. He lit the kerosene lantern and made two ice packs with plastic bags. He told Charlotte to sit on the sleeping bag and lean her back against the cabinet and let the ice do its work on her bruised palms.

I squiggle out of the sleeping bag and walk down the hallway. I see Charlotte cradling the ice packs in her palms. My father is standing in the opposite corner, not far from her because the kitchen is so small. He has his back against the counters where they meet at a right angle. I can see them because of the light from the kerosene lantern, but the hallway is dark and they haven't yet seen me. I am about to step into the kitchen when I hear Charlotte say, "You shouldn't blame Nicky for what happened today."

I stop.

"It was all my idea," Charlotte adds. "I begged her."

"She should have known better," my father says. "You both should have known better."

I turn away from the kitchen and put my back to the wall.

"It was awful," Charlotte says.

"I imagine it was," my father says.

I'm not sure what surprises me more — that my father and Charlotte are in the kitchen together or that they're actually talking.

"How're the hands?" I hear my father ask.

"A little numb," she says.

"Keep the ice on them. I should have told Nicky I was sleeping here before you both went to bed."

"I didn't see you."

I slide down the wall and sit on the floor. I draw my knees up to my chin.

"You warm enough?" my father asks.

"I'm all right," Charlotte says.

I imagine Charlotte with her head tilted back against the cabinets, possibly with her eyes closed.

"You'll be going tomorrow," my father says after a time. "The plow should get here in the afternoon."

There is a long silence in the kitchen.

"It was never our plan to abandon the baby," Charlotte says. "I want you to know that."

My father says nothing.

"James just kept saying, 'We'll take it one step at a time.' That's what he'd say whenever I'd mention the future. I thought he would know what to do when the time came. He'd worked in a hospital for a semester, and he was going to medical school."

I hear the clink of ice cubes in a plastic bag. I'm breathing so shallowly I have to take a gulp of air.

"I suppose you thought you loved him," my father says.

"I did love him," she says.

"You're how old?" my father asks.

"Nineteen."

"Old enough to think for yourself. Didn't it ever occur to you that you might be endangering the life of the child by not telling anyone beforehand?"

"You mean, like, a doctor," Charlotte says.

"Yes, a doctor."

"I thought about it," Charlotte says. "I went to the library and read about pregnancy and birth. I was sick during the early part of the summer. Morning sickness, except that it lasted all day. I was worried about that. But if I went to a doctor, I was afraid either my parents would find out or the school would."

"There are clinics," my father says.

It's cold in the hallway, and I don't have the sleeping bag. I draw myself together in a ball.

"I worked as a temp with an insurance agency," Charlotte says. "I moved from office to office, subbing for people who went on vacation. I was living with James by then. My parents thought I was sharing an apartment with another girl. Once they came to visit, and we had to put all of James's stuff in his car for the weekend. My father found an issue of *Sports Illustrated* in the bathroom, and I had to go on this riff about how I'd just become a baseball fan."

Charlotte pauses.

"In the fall," she continues, "I pretty much stopped going to my classes. I took long walks, and I learned to cook a couple of things."

"You were playing house," my father says dismissively.

"I suppose."

"Where do your parents live?"

Charlotte doesn't answer.

"I'm not going to call them, if that's what you're worried about," my father says.

"No, it's just that . . ."

"I'm not going to call in the police either," he adds. "If I were going to do that, I'd have done it already. That's a decision you're going to have to make."

In the hallway I begin to shiver from the cold. I want to blow on my hands, but I don't dare for fear of giving myself away. My father will be furious if he finds out I am listening.

"They live in Rutland," Charlotte says.

"Vermont?"

"Yes. They worked in a paper mill," Charlotte says. "They got laid off. Now my mother works at a drugstore, but my father's still unemployed."

"Paying for school must have been a struggle," he says.

"One of my brothers is helping. *Was* helping. And I had loans, though I probably don't anymore."

"And the car?"

"It was my brother's. His old one. He gave it to me."

"Where's the school?"

"UVM."

"You're a long way from Burlington," my father says.

I know where Burlington is. I've skied Stowe, which isn't far from the northern Vermont city.

"When the labor started," Charlotte says, "we got in the car. James wanted to get as far away from the college as possible. And then the labor stopped for a while, so we kept going. When it started up again, we looked for signs for a motel. That was James's plan. To go to a motel and have the baby ourselves. If there was any sign of trouble, James said, he'd make sure we'd be only a few minutes away from a hospital. But if we didn't have to go, why should we risk it?"

My father makes a sound of disgust.

"And yes," Charlotte says, "I guess I was playing house. I convinced myself that James and I would get married, and I'd have the baby, and we'd live in his apartment, and he'd go to medical school, and everything would be great. The fact that it was secret just made it . . . just made it seem all the more romantic."

I imagine my father shaking his head.

"And no matter what happened afterward," Charlotte says with a quaver in her voice, "or what happens from here on out . . ." She takes a breath to collect herself. "That will always be a good memory for me. The time I spent with her. With the baby. Because she was inside me, and I talked to her, and . . ."

I hear a rip of paper towel.

"I'm sorry," Charlotte says.

"Here, use this," I hear my father say.

Charlotte blows her nose. "Thank you," she says.

"Where's he from?" From the sound of my father's voice, it seems that he's leaning against the counter again.

"You won't . . . ?"

"I told you I wouldn't."

"His father's a doctor. They live just outside of Boston. I've never met them."

"He didn't want his parents to know."

"That's the thing he was most afraid of."

"How was he going to explain you and the baby? Eventually?"

"I don't know," she says.

My father clears his throat. "Are you thinking about trying to get the baby back?" he asks.

"Part of me wants to," Charlotte says.

"Can you take care of her?"

"No."

"I don't know the law," my father says. "I don't know if they would give her to you. Even after whatever happens in court."

"When she was inside me, I wanted her so much," Charlotte says.

"Charlotte," my father says, his voice low. It's the first time he has used her name, and it shocks me. "You have your whole life in front of you. No, don't look away. Listen to me. There will be consequences whatever you decide. Hard consequences. Things you'll have to live with for the rest of your life. But *think* first. Think about the baby, about what might be best for her. Maybe you should fight for her, I can't say. Only you can answer that."

"You lost a baby," Charlotte says with a kind of snap.

Her words send an electric zing through the air and around the corner to me. I wait for the sound of footsteps, for the sound of my father leaving the room.

"I'm sorry," Charlotte says at once. "I shouldn't have said that."

"It was different," my father says.

"Really, I'm sorry," Charlotte says.

"Very, very different."

"I know," Charlotte says, "I know. You weren't to blame. You didn't do anything. It just happened to you."

"You know about the accident," my father says.

"Yes. Nicky told me."

"Did she."

"Just the fact of it. That it happened."

I hear a creak from upstairs. Wood settling, my father once explained. Even after a hundred and fifty years, the house was still settling into the ground. Burrowing in.

"Maybe you should take those off now," my father says.

"I want to tell you what happened in the motel room," Charlotte says.

"I don't want to know."

"Please," she says. "I want you to understand."

"Why?"

"I don't know. You found her."

"Nicky's asleep?" my father asks.

"She was snoring when I got up."

My head snaps up. I snore?

"James and I drove a long way," Charlotte says. "I had to get out once. I couldn't hold it in anymore. I couldn't even make it to the woods. I just went on the snowbank. And then there was this terrible shuddering feeling, and I saw that there was blood and . . . other stuff on the snowbank . . . and I got scared, and I started yelling for James. He got out of the car and went white when he saw the blood. I couldn't get up, the pain from the contractions was so bad, so he hauled me up and got me in the car and we made it to the motel."

In the hallway I fold my hands like two fists under my chin. My eyes are wide open, even though there's nothing to see.

"There were maybe two other cars in the lot," Charlotte says. "Hardly anyone there at all. James went into the office while I stayed in the car. He told me not to yell, so I bit my hand. He came out and got me inside. I can hardly remember what the room looked like. There were these curtains. Green plaid. Ugly."

"I've seen the room," my father says.

"I lay down on the bed," she says. "The contractions were every minute or so. There was hardly any time in between. I was grunting. I thought because of the blood the baby would come fast, but it didn't. It felt like I was there for hours."

"You didn't think of getting to a hospital?" my father asks.

"I said once, 'I need to get to a hospital,' but the contractions were coming so fast, I thought I would deliver any minute, and I didn't want it to happen in the car. I was in so much pain, I didn't know how I'd even get to the car."

Charlotte pauses. "I didn't know what it would be like. What was normal to feel. I was scared to death. I thought I was going to die."

"And what was James doing all this time?"

"Sometimes he sat with me. I remember digging my fingernails into his arm when I was having a contraction. He paced. He'd bought some Demerol from a guy to have on hand for the pain, and he gave me two with a glass of water. And then when it got worse, he gave me two more. I didn't even care what the right dose was. I'd have taken a hundred of them. I just wanted the pain to go away."

I can hear my father sighing.

"I started wanting to push," Charlotte says. "I realized then that I couldn't get up from that bed and make it to the car. Whatever was going to happen was going to happen in that motel room. And that's when James really started to fall apart. He kept yelling, 'What are we going to do? I don't know what to do.' So I had to tell him. I had to talk him through it. I asked him if he could see the head. I made him wash his hands. I was just grunting then. I tried to breathe the way they say to in the books, but it didn't work."

I wrap my arms around my legs.

"And then I couldn't stop pushing, and the pain was just unbelievable," Charlotte says. "I felt as though I was being torn wide open. I was sure I was going to die. I yelled, and it's amazing someone didn't hear us."

In the kitchen there's a long silence.

"And then she was out," Charlotte says finally. "The baby was born. James was crying. I told him to pick the baby up and get the mucus out, and she cried right away. She was covered with that white stuff. James thought there was something wrong with her. I told him to cut the cord — the scissors were in my bag in a plastic bag — and he did. And then I told him to wrap her in a towel. I told him to watch for the placenta, the placenta had to come out. There was a lot of pain then, and this surprised me. I think something got torn. I was shivering, and I had a terrible headache."

There's another silence.

"I think that's when I realized how much James didn't want the baby," Charlotte says. "I really started to lose it then. I was crying. I told him to pick the baby up and hold her and to check for all her toes and fingers. He seemed calmer then. I said, 'Give her to me,' and he did. He just laid her across my stomach. I put my hand on her, but I was drifting by then, drifting in and out. I remember I propped myself up and looked at her. She had her face turned toward me. I had a tremendous feeling of relief. And then I lay back again, just resting for a second. And then I must have passed out."

"You passed out?" my father asks.

"The next thing I knew was James was in my face, and he was saying, 'Get up. We have to get out of here. We have to get you to the car.' And I said, 'Where's the baby?' and he said, 'She's in the car. She's sleeping in the basket we brought. But it's cold out there, and we have to get going.'

"He helped me up. I was sore and could hardly move. 'Walk like there's nothing wrong,' he said. He locked the door of the motel and kept the key. He put me in the passenger side. He opened the back door and bent over the basket like he was tucking the baby in, checking on her, and he said, 'She's sleeping now.' And I said, 'I have to feed her.' And he said, 'When she wakes up.' I remember I turned around, and I saw the basket mounded up with the blankets we'd brought, and I thought she was in there. I had to reach around to put my hand on the blankets. James put the key in the ignition and started the car. I drifted off again. I woke once, I don't know how far we'd gone, and I said, 'She's still sleeping?' and he said, 'Yes.' That was all. Just 'Yes.'

"And then I fell asleep again."

"You never saw her," my father says.

"Just that one time when she was on my stomach," Charlotte says.

"Then what happened?" my father asks, his voice steady, even a little relentless.

"When we pulled into the driveway of our apartment, I woke up. I said, 'Get the baby. Maybe something's wrong. I don't hear her.' And James said, 'She woke up once. You were sleeping. She's fine.' And I said, 'She did?' And he said, 'Let's get you in first. Then I'll get the baby.'

"So he came around to my side and helped me out and up the steps and into the apartment, and all the time, I'm saying, 'I'm fine, just get the baby.' He helped me get my coat off and I sat down on the sofa, and he went out to get the baby, and that was that."

The silence is long, and I think that maybe Charlotte has finished her story.

"I must have drifted off again for a few minutes," Charlotte says after a time, "because when I woke up, James was sitting across from me, and he was crying."

Charlotte's voice is so low now, I have to strain to hear her.

"I knew right away it was terrible. I started saying,

'What is it? What is it?' And James told me the baby had died. 'It's not true!' I said. 'I heard her cry.' He said she was alive for a few minutes, but that she died. He said he tried to revive her, he did CPR or something, but that she was dead. He said he panicked and wrapped her up in a towel and took her out behind the motel and left her body in a sleeping bag he had in the trunk.

"I went crazy. I hit him in the face. I fell on the floor. 'She might have been alive,' I kept screaming.

"'No,' he said, 'she wasn't.'

"'Then what was in the basket?' I yelled. And he said, 'Nothing.' And I said, 'Why didn't you tell me?' And he said, 'I thought you'd go crazy and I wouldn't be able to get you into the car. I wanted to get you home first.'

"And I said, 'Home? I'd rather be dead.'"

In the hallway I bend my forehead to my knees.

"And then I realized that James was crying, too, just as much as I was, and that really scared me because then I believed him. I knew it was all true, and, oh God, I was so sad. . . ."

I wrap my arms around my head.

"'It's punishment,' I said to James," Charlotte continues. "'Punishment for what?' James said. 'For doing it the way we did. For not telling anyone. For not going to a hospital. If we'd gone to a hospital, she'd be alive.' He said we didn't know that. But I was sure of it. It just made it all so much worse.

"He stayed with me that night and most of the next day. But then he said he had to go home to his parents. It was Christmas break, and he'd already had to make too many excuses why he wasn't home yet. I said I'd be fine. I wanted him to go. I just wanted to be alone. James packed his duffle bag and said good-bye, and I remember that we didn't even kiss. I remember thinking, *This means something.* I knew he wanted to get away from me just as much as I wanted him to go." She pauses. "He didn't love me, did he?"

"No," my father says.

"You wouldn't do this to someone you loved, would you?"

"No, you wouldn't."

Charlotte begins to cry again. After a time, I hear her blow her nose. "About an hour later, I walked into the bedroom to lie down, and the radio was on. I remember this surprised me. I didn't have the energy to walk around the bed and turn it off. I just climbed in and pulled the covers over my head. When the news came on, I heard something about an abandoned baby being in stable condition. I sat up. The announcer said Shepherd, New Hampshire. I hadn't known the name of the town where the motel was. I had a map of New England in my car. I went out to get it. I looked up where Shepherd was. I ran back in and got my keys and drove to the store and bought a newspaper. There was a story in it about the baby. I was just so happy. So happy she wasn't dead." Charlotte pauses. "And that's when it hit me. I realized what James had done. *He'd left her to die.* At first I couldn't believe it. I told myself that he'd just made a horrible mistake. He'd thought she was dead but she wasn't really. And then slowly I realized he had to have known she was alive, and still he'd traipsed out into the snow and left her there. I could hardly breathe. I didn't cry. I couldn't scream. It was just nothing."

"He did it deliberately," my father says. "He knew she was alive."

Charlotte is silent.

"He planned it all along," my father says.

"I don't know," Charlotte says. "Maybe he just panicked. I can't believe he drove all that way, knowing he was going to kill her."

"Why didn't you call the police?"

"I was afraid," Charlotte says. "If I went to the police, I knew I'd be charged with attempted murder. I was scared. So I began to think, Well, it's okay now, isn't it? She's alive, and someone will take care of her. I couldn't take care of her. I had no money. I would have to leave James's apartment. I couldn't go home to my family with a baby. So it was all right, wasn't it?"

My father is silent.

"I called James at his home," Charlotte says. "He wasn't there. His mother said he'd gone skiing with friends."

"Skiing?" my father asks, incredulous.

"I was so dumbfounded I just hung up the phone."

"Incredible," my father says.

"I lay in bed for a week," Charlotte says. "I hardly ate anything. I was so tired. Finally I got up and drove myself to the library and looked up all the back issues of the newspapers until I came to a story with your name in it." She pauses. "And then I drove here."

"Why?"

"I had to see you."

"I don't understand."

"What was my life worth if I didn't thank you?" Charlotte says.

Her extraordinary question — almost more amazing than her confession, almost more astonishing than her terrible story — floats through the kitchen and out to the hallway. A pulse in my left ear begins to pound.

"I'd better go back to bed," Charlotte says. I can hear rustling, a soft thump against the cabinet. "My leg has fallen asleep."

"Give it a shake."

"It must be hard for you to hear this," Charlotte says.

"It would be a hard story for anyone to listen to," my father says.

"Look, I'm really sorry about what I said about losing a child."

"That's all right," my father says.

"I keep thinking I could have stopped him," Charlotte says.

A bomb explodes, one without sound. I bring my hand to my eyes, temporarily blinded by the light. Our house begins to hum.

"Oh!" Charlotte says, startled.

"The power's back," my father announces, sounding a little stunned himself.

I squint in the overbright light. The wood floor shines, and there's a glare off the painted wall. I want to shut my eyes. The world is harsh and ugly, and I hate it.

I scoot along the floor and crawl into my sleeping bag. When Charlotte enters the room, I prop myself up. "What happened?" I ask, squinting up at her.

"The power's on," she says. The palms of her hands are bright red. Her nose is pink and raw, and her voice is thick.

"Weird," I say.

"It's the middle of the night," she says. "Do you want me to turn off the light so you can go back to sleep?"

"Where were you?"

"I got up to get some milk."

"What happened to your hands?"

"I tripped over your father," she says. She turns off the light and crawls into the sleeping bag beside me.

I slide back into my own bag. I press my hand against

my chest to keep my heart from jumping out of my skin. I think about everything Charlotte told my father — the blood on the snow, the way Charlotte kept passing out, the moment she realized James had left the baby to die. It was all too awful, too horrible. I cover my face with my hands.

And then I begin to think about how my father and I drove north from New York and settled in a town called Shepherd. Charlotte and James drove south from Burlington and found a random motel in Shepherd. Our paths crossed at a single spot in the woods. But what if, I wonder, on the second day of our trip, my father and I had figured out the complicated interchange at White River Junction and gone north as we were supposed to do? What if my father had decided to make a go of it in New York after all? What if my mother had dropped a quarter at the register when she was buying a present for her parents at the mall and knelt to retrieve it, thus delaying her two seconds to her car? What if my father had not, as my mother had once told me, walked into the university library one spring morning to read about the Yankees-Orioles game the night before and seen my mother at the circulation desk, studying for a chemistry exam while putting in her work-study hours, and asked her, on the spur of the moment, how he might get permission to look at a series of rare Jefferson drawings kept in the vault?

I would not exist. My father and mother would not have married. There would have been no Clara.

I want to believe that my father and I were meant to stumble across Baby Doris and give her a chance at life. But now I'm not so sure. I am thinking about accidents and intersecting footsteps as I drift off to sleep.

Six days after Clara was born, she developed a cough and a fever. My mother took her to the pediatrician, who prescribed a mild antibiotic and cool baths which made my sister howl. Her temperature came down, and my mother thought the worst was over. That afternoon I went into my parents' room to see Clara, who was sleeping on her back, her body uncovered but for a diaper. My mother, who hadn't eaten since the evening before, had gone downstairs to make herself a bowl of soup. I sat on my parents' bed and gazed at the crib, Clara's tiny body moving in and out of focus depending upon whether I stared at the wooden bars of the railing or at her. The crib sheet and comforter were of pastel checks; a threadbare duck we called Quack-Quack was perched in a corner. Quack-Quack was remarkably intact but for the missing plush on one side of his face. I actually thought he looked a little creepy and was glad when Clara inherited him. As I watched, I let my eyes focus on Clara, and I noticed that her stomach, below her rib cage, compressed with each breath. I hadn't known this about babies before, and I thought it fascinating. It was as though her skin were a thin rubber membrane and someone was sucking the air out her back. I observed this for a few minutes more, and it suddenly occurred to me that this might not be normal. I went to the top of the stairs and called my mother.

"Mom?"

I could hear her in the kitchen.

"Mom?" I yelled again.

"What?" she asked from the bottom of the stairs.

"Clara's stomach is doing something weird," I said.

Perhaps I had noticed it because I was eye level with my sister. Or maybe it was only because I was bored and had nothing to do. My mother came running up the stairs. "See?" I pointed. "The way it goes up and down?"

"You're right," she said, at first not understanding its significance. "I'll call Dr. Blake."

She sat on the bed and made the call. She was in the middle of describing Clara's condition when she was interrupted. She sat up straight. "Yes," she said. "Right away."

She hung up and called for an ambulance.

"Mom?" I asked. "What is it?"

"It's okay," she said. "We just have to get Clara checked

out." She picked Clara up and held her head against her shoulder. "Grab the diaper bag," she said.

"What's happening?" I asked.

"We're waiting for an ambulance," she said.

"To go to the hospital?"

"Yes."

"Why don't we just drive there?"

"Dr. Blake said not to, that this is the fastest way."

My mother paced by the front door, peering out the sidelights from time to time. I stood with my jacket on and the diaper bag slung over my shoulder. Within minutes we heard the siren.

Neither my mother nor I was allowed to go with the medics. My mother handed the baby over, and it wouldn't be until years later that I'd understand how hard that was for her to do. After the rear doors of the ambulance were shut, my mother ran for her car, the green VW. "Get in," she yelled to me.

My mother, a ridiculously cautious driver — sometimes to the point of exasperation on the part of her passenger, usually me — backed out of the driveway in one shot and left rubber as she raced after the ambulance. She took the Bug to its max, straining the engine, so that she could keep the ambulance in sight. I held on to the door handle and tried not to speak, because my mother, under the best of circumstances, was not an expert driver. Usually she sat forward, hunched over the wheel, looking behind her in both directions before she dared to change lanes, a practice I never saw my father do. But that day my mother was a pro.

She abandoned the VW, door open, at the emergency entrance and ran after the gurney that held Clara, whose cries we could hear receding. I followed my mother, the oversized bag flapping against my thigh and slowing me down. I knew it was serious as soon as I saw the doctor hovering over the gurney. Clara was wheeled into a cubicle with white curtains on either side. She was put inside a metal box, which struck me as bizarre and my mother as horrifying. "Can't I at least hold her?" my mother begged.

"Step aside, Mrs. Dillon," the doctor said.

"If I nurse her, she'll stop crying," my mother said.

"Nursing her right now would be the worst possible thing you could do," he said.

I didn't like the doctor, who seemed bossy and self-important and barked at the nurses around him. He treated my mother as an annoying object that was simply in the way.

"Is it bad?" she asked.

"Your baby can't breathe," the doctor said.

I stood against the wall on the far side of the room. I let the diaper bag fall to the ground.

"Nicky, here's two quarters," my mother said, standing in front of me. "Go find a pay phone and call your father. You know the number?"

I did. I sometimes called him from home after school if I had a math problem I couldn't solve.

"Do it now," she said.

I picked up the diaper bag and searched for a pay phone. A woman sitting behind a desk gave me directions, and I finally found a bank of phones near an elevator. "Dad, you better come," I said.

"Why?" he asked, and I could hear alarm in his voice.

"Clara can't breathe," I said.

"Where are you?" he asked.

"At the hospital where she was born."

"Tell your mother I'll be right there."

I sat by the wall, a buffer of nurses and curtains shielding me from Clara. She was moved to another part of the hospital, and I moved with the entourage. Sometime that night my mother looked over in my direction and said, "Rob, she's green."

My father came over and sat beside me.

"She's going to die, isn't she?" I asked.

"Of course not," he said.

"Then why is there so much fuss?"

"That's the way hospitals are," he said.

I knew this wasn't true. When I'd broken my wrist the year before, we'd had to wait for two hours in the emergency room, until my father finally lost his temper and started yelling at the triage nurse that his daughter was in pain.

"I'll call Jeff and Mary," my father said, referring to a couple my parents were friendly with and who lived near the hospital. "You can eat and watch TV, and I'll come get you later."

That night the doctors worked on Clara for hours. She had a not-uncommon but life-threatening form of infant pneumonia. My mother was told that Clara might not make it through the night, a fact I wouldn't learn until later. At Jeff and Mary's, I ate pizza and stayed up late watching TV. I slept in a guest room in a shirt that belonged to Mary. In the morning Jeff took me to my house so I could change and go to school. When we arrived the front door was open and the house was freezing. A newspaper my mother had set on the coffee table had blown all over the room. Jeff made me wait outside while he moved through all the rooms in a crouch like the cops do on TV. He returned and reported that the house was empty and that nothing had been disturbed. Even so, I was afraid to step over the threshold. Jeff had to persuade me that my mother, as she was running to the ambulance, had forgotten to shut the door. I made Jeff come upstairs with me and stand outside my room anyway while I changed my clothes.

Clara was in the hospital for three days, during which my mother never left her side. My father went to work in the mornings only, so that he'd be home when I got off the bus. Together we'd travel to the hospital, more relaxed the second day than the first, more relaxed the third day than the second. On the third night, we came home with Clara, who weighed two pounds less than she had when she'd left the house. She looked scrawny, like a plucked bird. Every so often during that week and the next, my mother and father would look at each other, sigh, and then shake their heads, as if to say, *That was a close one.*

"You may have saved your sister's life," my mother said once to me.

I wake at daybreak. From my vantage point on the floor, I see something I haven't seen in days, a powder-blue sky shot through with pink silk. Beside me, Charlotte sleeps. Even my father seems not to be up.

Daybreak comes fast in northern New England. I know that the sun will rise within minutes if not seconds. I wait, snug in my bag. I remember the events of the night before. A story was told. In the daylight it seems impossible.

The sun rises over the top of Bott Hill and lights up the snow-covered woods and meadows with such an intense pink light that I slide out of my sleeping bag to see. The color spills slowly across the landscape, and for the first time in my life, I wish I had a camera. I know that we once owned one — I can remember my father taking that picture of me holding Clara on my mother's bed, and there are certainly many other photographs in my album to prove it — but I haven't seen it out since we moved to New Hampshire. Like everything else from our former lives, the reminder of family photographs has been too difficult for my father to manage. But that morning, for the three or four minutes that the snow is on fire, I want one. I make a square with my thumbs and forefingers and stand at the window framing shots and making barely audible clicks with my tongue. Then so fast that it seems like a trick, the lovely pink is gone, and the snow is white and bright and hard to look at. The sky deepens to the chrome blue of postcards. Only the tall pines show green.

Charlotte is still snoring lightly on the floor. Maybe everybody snores. I think it amazing that she can sleep at all — the den is lit brighter than it has been in weeks, maybe a year. And lit bright, it shows its dust: the dust of ashes on the hearth; a fine layer of ordinary dust on the coffee table; a weird, weblike dust on the lamp shades. The sun makes oblongs of high reality on the floor and rug and on Charlotte, who rolls over and turns her face away.

In the kitchen I find cornmeal and flour and baking powder and eggs. I mix the ingredients in a bowl and wait for the pan to heat up. I move easily between counter and stove. I wonder if dark stories can be told with the sun streaming through the windows. I sprinkle raspberries, like seeds, onto the circles of batter. The raspberries were frozen in the summer, and we have bags and bags of them in a freezer in the basement. I'll mash and mix some of them with sugar and serve them in a small pitcher to pour over the pancakes.

I fetch the trays from the top of the fridge and begin to set them up. The batter sizzles in the hot oil. My pancakes are always crispy; the secret is the cornmeal.

Finding room to lay the trays down is a problem as usual. I set one across the sink, another on a pile of books. Charlotte appears in the doorway.

She has removed my father's clothes and has on her wrinkled white blouse and jeans. Her face is pink and creased with sleep. Her hair, uncombed, separates at one ear. She hugs her arms. "I rolled the bags," she says.

In the other doorway, as if summoned, my father appears as well. His hair is spiked in all directions. He has on a maroon sweatshirt and a pair of tan moccasins, frayed at the heel. For a moment all I can think about is my father and Charlotte in the kitchen together last night.

"Hi," he says. He looks the same as he did yesterday. I realize I've been expecting a different father, a different Dad.

"Good morning," he says to Charlotte.

"Good morning," she says back to him.

I glance from Charlotte to my father and back again. Do I see an acknowledgment pass between them, or do I only imagine it?

"Pancakes," my father says. "Good. I'm starved."

He takes the pot from under the Mr. Coffee and fills it with water.

"What can I do?" Charlotte asks.

"Nothing, really," I say. I pause. I have an idea.

"Watch these," I say to my father, indicating the frying pan. "I just put them in. I'll be right back. Charlotte, come with me."

Charlotte follows me into the front room, lit just as bright as the other rooms. I touch a walnut dining table — oval and beautifully finished.

"What are we doing?" she asks.

"We're going to lift this off and carry it into the kitchen," I say. "Take that end."

Together Charlotte and I maneuver the tabletop through the kitchen door and prop it up against the cabinets.

My father studies us, spatula in hand.

Charlotte walks with me to the front room again and helps me bring the bottom structure into the kitchen. We set that down as well and then lift the tabletop onto it. The table takes up most of the kitchen. For us to be able to cook and wash dishes, a good third of it will have to stick out into the passageway between the den and the back hallway. But we have a table in the kitchen.

"Well," my father says.

I set the plates and the silverware and glasses on the

table and store the trays over the fridge. I bring out two chairs from the front room and get the third from my bedroom. I pour orange juice in glasses and fill a white pitcher with raspberry syrup.

My father sits at the head of the table, Charlotte and I across from each other. For a few seconds the three of us look at one another and at the stack of pancakes, as if we are a family pondering whether or not to say grace. Sitting at a table in our kitchen feels both strange and familiar. It is a simple thing, but my father and I have gone a long time without it.

I look at the place on the kitchen floor where Charlotte was sitting last night. I remember the clink of ice cubes, the small circle of light from the lantern. I remember all these sights and sounds, but the words I heard last night seem part of a dream.

"These are good," Charlotte says.

I pick up my fork and take a bite. I decide I like having my plate on a stable surface, being able to shift my legs while eating. I enjoy the sight of the small white pitcher of raspberry syrup against the dark wood. For the second time that day, I wish I had a camera.

"This is a beautiful table," Charlotte says after a time.

"My father taught me the rudiments of carpentry when I was fourteen," my father says. "I helped him build a house."

I didn't know this fact. I examine my father. There

might be whole universes of facts about him I don't know. "When's Grammie's plane?" I ask.

"Two thirty," my father says.

I stir my hot chocolate. The marshmallows are little cardboard pellets. I know that if I drink the cocoa, I'll be sick.

"You have a present for her?" my father asks.

"I made her a necklace," I say.

I hear a sound that at first I can't identify. I hold my breath and listen. The sound is faint — a motor, but more than a motor, a motor that grinds and then scrapes, grinds and then scrapes. I set down my spoon. It's a sound as unwelcome in that still and silent world as a tank rolling into a village it's about to level.

"Harry," my father says.

"He's too soon," I say.

"I'll go out to him," my father says.

Our road is the last on Harry's route. It's not unusual for my father to greet him with a mug of coffee or, if it's really late in the day, with a beer. Once Harry came into the house to use the bathroom, and he stayed talking to my father with a Beck's in his hand for an hour. He's a local who makes his living in the winter plowing for the town and for private individuals. There's no shortage of work in New Hampshire in the winter.

Charlotte sips the last of her coffee. She sets the mug down.

I feel a panicky sensation in my chest.

"I guess I'll go upstairs and make up the bed," Charlotte says. "Do you have clean sheets so I can put them on for your grandmother?"

"Why?"

"She's coming, isn't she?"

"I don't know where the clean sheets are," I say, though I do: they're in the top drawer of the bureau.

"I'll just strip the bed then," she says, standing.

I have an image of Charlotte ripping the sheets from the bed, leaving a bare mattress. "You can't leave," I say.

"I have to," she says.

"You could live with us. What would be wrong with that? We could say you're my cousin and that you're living with us for a while. You could get a job, save money, go back to college."

Charlotte gives a quick shake of her head.

"But I've got it all worked out," I wail.

"If the police discover me here, you and your father will be accomplices."

That word again. "I don't care," I say. And it's true, I don't care. I *want* to be an accomplice to Charlotte's life.

I watch as Charlotte takes her dishes to the sink. She rinses them carefully. She wipes her hands on a dish towel. She slips past my chair and heads for the stairs.

For a minute I sit alone at the table. I touch its surface and remember Charlotte in the front room that first day, running her fingers along the furniture. I hear Charlotte upstairs, and I have again an image of a stripped mattress, blankets and sheets neatly folded.

I find my jacket in the back hallway. When Harry has gone, I'll plead with my father. We can't just send Charlotte away, I'll tell him; we can't.

Harry is sitting in his truck, his window rolled down, a mug of coffee in his hand. My father is standing next to him. "Hey there," Harry says to me when I reach my father's side.

"Hi," I say.

"Getting ready for Christmas?" he asks in that jovial way adults speak to children.

"Guess so."

Harry, older than my father, has a thin beard and an even thinner ponytail. His truck is covered with Pink Floyd stickers. Behind Harry is a neat four-foot-wide path the plow has made, the snow at the right edge piled high. He'll get the other side of the drive on his way down.

"You're early today," my father says.

"Been out all night. Got the call around ten."

"You must be wrecked."

"Nah, I'm fine," Harry says, adjusting his baseball hat. Red Sox. "Headed home to put up the tree."

"How many inches did we get?"

"I can tell you exactly. Forty-one."

"Must be rough, plowing with the ice underneath."

"You want me to go up to the barn?" he asks.

"No," my father says, "we're okay. I stayed with it. Just do this little bit here we didn't shovel."

Harry hands my father the empty mug and puts his truck in gear. He cocks a finger at me. "Don't forget the beer and cookies for Santa," he says.

My father and I back away. Harry lowers the plow. We watch as he makes a wide swath. "Dad," I say.

"Don't start."

"She has nowhere to go."

"She has places."

"We just can't send her away."

"She's a big girl. She'll be all right."

Harry turns around, works his way back to us. He gives a wave out his window as he heads down the long drive.

"Dad, please?"

My father walks away from me to the side of the barn. He takes a glance, seems satisfied, and turns in the direction of the house. I follow to see what he was looking at. His truck and Charlotte's car are entirely shoveled out, a fine dusting of snow on top. It's what my father was doing all night — making sure Charlotte could leave in the morning.

Charlotte is standing in the hallway when my father and I enter the house. She has her parka and her boots on. Her pocketbook is slung over her shoulder.

No.

"I guess I'd better get going," she says.

"Give Harry another minute or so to get all the way down the drive," my father says. "Give me your keys. I'll go warm up your car."

Charlotte reaches into her pocket and takes out her keys.

"Stop it!" I yell. "Just stop it."

My father seems startled, more by the pitch of my voice than by what I've said. He stands motionless for a moment and then opens the door and steps out.

Charlotte smoothes my hair out of the collar of my parka. "Keep up the knitting," she says lightly.

"I don't want you to go," I say.

"I'll be fine," she says.

"You won't be fine. And how am I going to know where you are? Will you write to me? Or call me?"

"Of course, I'll write to you."

"But you don't know our address. You have to have our address." I run into the kitchen and find a paper napkin and a ballpoint pen. I write down my address and phone number in my best printing. I add my name just in case she forgets who the address belongs to.

"I'm glad I met you," Charlotte says when I give it to her. "I'm glad I came here."

"But I want you to *live* here," I say helplessly.

"I can't," she says. "You know that." She taps her teeth. "When do these come off?" she asks.

"April," I say.

"You'll be beautiful," she says, smiling.

I hear the sound of an engine. I watch as my father brings Charlotte's car around to the side of the house. Steam rises up from the blue sedan.

"I hate good-byes," I say. "Why is everybody always leaving me?"

My father enters the house, stomps his boots against the mat. He hands Charlotte her car keys. I refuse to look at him.

"Thank you," Charlotte says, "for everything."

"Be careful on the hill," my father says. "It's plowed, but it'll be slick. And take it slow on the streets."

Charlotte extends her hand, and my father shakes it.

"All right then," he says.

Charlotte tilts her head. I reach out for her arm. She lets me hug her. I can feel her body beneath the padding of her jacket. I can smell her yeasty scent. Charlotte pulls away, and then she is gone.

I run to the window and press my face against it. I watch as Charlotte walks to her car. She opens the car door and slips inside.

"This is all wrong!" I cry.

Charlotte sits in the car a moment. Maybe she's adjusting the temperature or the radio. Maybe she's putting on her gloves. As she does, I remember the necklace of blue fire-polished beads she made the night before. I have to give it to her; she doesn't even know I finished it.

I find it in the box in the den. Through the window, I can see the blue sedan moving slowly forward now, as if Charlotte were testing the snowy drive for traction. I run to the back door and fling it open. "Wait!" I call out after her.

I run in stocking feet along the drive. I hold the necklace aloft, hoping she will glance into her rearview mirror and see it. "Stop!" I yell. "Charlotte, please stop!"

In the center of the driveway, Harry has plowed down to a layer of ice. When I hit that icy patch, I skid in my stocking feet, my arms flailing to keep me upright. I come to an abrupt stop where the ice is once again covered with snow. I stumble forward three or four enormous steps and then catch my balance.

When I look up, the blue sedan has pulled away from the house — too far for me to catch it now.

Through the trees, where the long driveway bends, I see a blur of red. I watch as a man steps out to the middle of the drive. I see a flicker of brake lights as Charlotte stops her car.

On the morning of the accident, I packed a blue nylon backpack for my sleepover at Tara's. I also had a small plastic pouch, courtesy of Delta Airlines, that held a folded toothbrush, a tiny tube of toothpaste, a comb, a pair of socks, and an eyeshade. Though I'd gone to several sleepovers that fall, I hadn't yet used the pouch. Extravagantly, I decided to take it with me that night.

I dressed in pink corduroy overalls and a purple shirt. When I got downstairs, my mother was sitting by the kitchen table. She had on a ratty old plaid bathrobe that smelled of Mom even when she wasn't in it. The shoulder had unidentifiable stains on it, most of which I attributed to Clara. My mother had smudged mascara below her eyes, and her hair was flattened on one side. Beneath the robe, she was wearing a pale blue nylon nightgown as well as a pair of thick white socks that were getting brown on the bottoms. Clara, apparently, was still asleep.

A bowl, a spoon, a glass of juice, and a Flintstones vitamin were set at my place at the table. I poured Cheerios into the bowl.

"You all packed?" my mother asked.

"Yup."

"Don't forget to say thank you," she said.

"Mom, I haven't even gone yet."

"Even so," she said. "And make your bed. Always make your bed."

"We sleep on the floor."

"Then roll your sleeping bag."

"Okay," I said.

My mother took a sip of tea. "You have your lunch money?"

"No."

She got up and took three quarters from a paper cup in a cabinet. "We'll pick you up at ten," she said.

"Ten?"

"Nana and Poppy are coming tomorrow to celebrate Christmas with us early, before they go to Florida."

I looked around. "Where's Dad?"

"He'll be right down. He got a late start."

From upstairs I could hear the rapid padding of feet into the bedroom from the bathroom.

"Are your presents wrapped?" my mother asked.

"Not yet."

"You can do that tomorrow, too."

"Everybody stays until eleven," I said. "Mrs. Rice makes a big breakfast for all of us."

"Ten," my mother said.

I remember that she stood and watered a plant on the sill over the sink. My father came down the stairs smelling of Neutrogena shampoo. He drank his coffee standing up. "You seen my keys?" he asked my mother.

"They're on the dining room table."

"You ready, Freddy?" he asked me, goosing me at the back of the neck.

I put on my jacket. My mother bent down to give me a hug. "Be a good girl," she said. "I love you."

"I always *am,*" I said, annoyed.

We left the house, and I didn't look back. I didn't notice if my mother was still standing in the doorway, holding her robe closed at the neck. Maybe she waved or maybe she went upstairs to have a shower before Clara woke up. I didn't say *I love you, too,* to my mother. I didn't say goodbye to Clara. I don't know if my sister was sleeping on her stomach, arms and legs splayed, her diaper making a tight package under her sleeping suit, or if she had wormed her way into a corner as she sometimes did, clutching a white crocheted blanket to her chin. I don't know if Quack-Quack was with her in the crib. I don't even know for sure when it was I last saw Clara — at supper on my father's knee, or in her crib as I passed by on my way to the bathroom?

I was off to school, and I didn't look back. I had a date that night at Tara's.

A deputy comes to the house to inform us that Charlotte has been taken to Concord in a cruiser. Charlotte's car will be towed to the Shepherd police station. Neither of us is to leave the house. A police officer will be with us shortly to question us.

"Where's Detective Warren?" my father asks.

"He's gone to Concord with the young woman," the deputy says.

My father shuts the door and stands with his hand still on the knob. *This can't be happening to us,* I think. I have not said this to myself at any time since we found the baby.

"She'll think you called the police," I say.

My father stands rooted to the spot.

"*Did* you call the police?" I ask.

"No."

"Then do something!" I yell.

He takes his hand off the doorknob.

"You know she didn't know!" I shout. "You know she didn't do it!"

My father turns to look at me, a question on his face.

"I overheard you talking in the kitchen," I say.

"You heard all of it?"

"I heard every single word," I say defiantly.

"Nicky," he says.

"Charlotte fell asleep. She was on drugs. She didn't know what James was doing. It's not fair."

"She knew what he'd done when she got home," he says.

"She was scared," I say. "She was sick."

"She could have called the police."

"Would you have done that? When you were nineteen, would you have called the police?"

He unzips his jacket, tosses it to the bench. "I'd like to think I would have."

"Well, if you don't do something now," I yell, "they're going to put her in jail. She'll never get her baby back."

"Is that what this is all about?" my father asks, kicking off his boots.

"No," I say. "It's about saving Charlotte."

I'm vaguely aware of an exaggerated sense of drama, of a language my father and I never use. "You have to do the right thing," I say evenly. "You just have to."

"Nothing I can say will make any difference at all."

I glance down at the necklace in my hands. I whip it as hard as I can in his direction.

The necklace hits him in the jaw. From the way he brings his hand to his cheek, I can tell that it stings. "Nicky," he says, more bewildered than angry.

"Charlotte made that," I say. "And now she'll never have it. So you have it."

My father takes a step forward, but I hold my ground. He removes his hand from his cheek. There's a red mark where the necklace hit him. "Go to your room," he says.

"No."

"That's enough," he says, his voice more stern now.

"No, I won't go to my room," I say, "and there's nothing you can do to make me."

And suddenly I know that this is true. There's nothing my father can do to make me go to my room. The realization is both exhilarating and terrifying.

"You're just weak, you know that?" I say, putting my hands on my hips. "You're afraid to go to the police station. You're afraid to go anywhere. You just hide from the world."

"Nicky, don't," he says.

"You just retreat from the world like a coward." A thrilling kind of terror runs along my spine. I have never spoken to my father like this.

"There are reasons," he says.

"Oh really?" I ask. "Well, just in case you want to know, I lost my mother and sister, too."

My father briefly shuts his eyes. I wait for his face to close up on me in that terrible way it does — the eyes vacant, seeing only images from the past. For a time neither of us says a word.

"I know you did," he says.

"You're not living a normal life, Dad."

"I do the best I can."

I thrust my face forward. "But *I* don't have a normal life," I say. "How do you think it feels to be me? No friends to the house. No TV. We never go anywhere. You never answer the phone. We didn't even *have* a phone for six months because you didn't want to talk to anyone. And why did you give that Steve guy the wrong number, huh? Because you didn't want him calling you. That's sick, Dad. It's just sick."

"You want too much," he says.

"I just want my life back! Is that too much to ask?" I don't want to be crying — it ruins all arguments — but I am.

"You can't have that life back," he says.

I've gone too far — I know I have — but I can't stop myself. "I could have *some* life at least," I protest.

My father turns to look out the window. He puts a hand to the woodwork to support his weight. "A hundred times I've regretted the move," he says.

"We could have stayed in New York," I say.

"You were young, and I thought you'd get over it quickly."

"Well, I didn't," I say.

"I always thought you were doing pretty well," he says.

"I just pretend," I say. "For your sake."

He turns to me, surprised now. "You pretend?" he asks. "All this time you've been pretending?"

"So you wouldn't be sad," I say. "I can't stand it when you're sad."

My father bites the inside of his cheek. I can see that I've hurt him.

"Are you just trying to stay sad?" I ask. "To hold on to Mom and Clara?"

My father doesn't answer me.

"Because, Dad, here's the thing," I say. *I can't take care of you anymore!"*

My father looks away. A white noise rushes into my ears. With deliberately slow movements he puts his boots back on and reaches for his jacket. In three strides he is out the door.

I fall onto the bench, lightheaded and breathless.

I won't run after my father, I decide.

The sun beats in through the windows of the back hallway. It has grown warm with the solar heat. My socks are soaked at the soles, and I take them off.

I won't apologize.

I pick up the necklace and hoist myself up the banister of the stairs as if I weighed two hundred pounds. I walk to my room and lie on my back on my bed.

My stomach hurts. I ate too many pancakes. I turn onto my side, cradling my abdomen with my hands. It occurs to me to wonder where the promised police officer is. Will my father and I be arrested? I try to imagine that. My father and me in handcuffs, being led to a cruiser. My father and me sitting shackled side by side. It's too weird to contemplate. What would we say to each other? And then there would be the drive to the police station. Warren would be waiting for us at the other end, a smirk on his face. He'd won, hadn't he? And then my father and I would be separated, and I'd be led to a jail cell by a matron who looked like Mrs. Dean at school, thick all over. Would Charlotte be in a cell near me? Would we be able to speak to each other? Would we have to invent a code that we tapped through the walls? And why oh why did I eat so many pancakes? The cramps in my stomach are intense.

I think about my father, alone in the barn. Is he furious, kicking lumber and snapping tools down hard upon his workbench? Or is it worse than that? Is he sitting in his chair, in the Dad position, just staring out at the snow? If my stomach didn't hurt so much, I think I would go out to him now. I don't know what I'd say, but I'd try to tell him that I know he's done the best job he could. That I don't pretend all the time. That, actually, I'm usually pretty okay.

I get up to go to the bathroom. I vow never to eat pancakes again. It will be my New Year's resolution: never eat pancakes. I stop at the sink and study my reflection in the mirror. My skin is white, and I look sick. I try to smile, but all I see is metal. I turn away from the mirror, unzip my jeans, and sit on the toilet.

My head snaps up. Is it possible?

I examine my underwear again.

It's just a tiny stain, but it's unmistakably blood.

Maybe it's only coincidence. Or maybe it was the fight that brought it on. More likely it was simply time. But it's hard, in those confusing and exhilarating initial moments, not to think of it as something Charlotte has passed on to me. I remember my mother and feel a pang, but it's Charlotte I most want to tell.

I'll tell my grandmother when she gets to the house. She might cry. And I'll tell Jo the day after Christmas, when we go skiing. I imagine her squeal. Bit by bit I'll let others know, or Jo will. My father will see the box of Kotex in the bathroom and think Charlotte left it there. He'll put it away. I'll take it out again and set it on the sink, giving him the hint. Eventually he'll get the picture without my ever having to say a word. I wonder if there will be a moment when he'll look at me differently, and if he does, if I will see it. I hope it doesn't make him sad, sad for my mother who is not here to see me reach this milestone.

I have had enough sadness to last a lifetime.

I didn't see Charlotte leave with the box of Kotex. I search the bathroom closet. There are squeezed-out tubes of toothpaste and little slivers of soap, but no Kotex. I walk into the guest room and open the closet door, and there on the upper shelf is the box, half-hidden behind a woolly blanket with a satin edge. I reach for the box and return to the bathroom, and though uninitiated, figure out the not-too-difficult process of securing a pad.

I look in the mirror again. *I am a woman,* I say to my reflection, trying it out.

Who am I kidding? I'm just a twelve-year-old girl waiting for a policeman to come and arrest her. I still have cramps, but knowing that I'm not going to be sick makes the pain more bearable. I try to remember what it is Jo always takes when she has cramps at school. I find some Motrin in the medicine cabinet and take two.

I hear a sound I would know anywhere. I know I have only sixty seconds to make it to the passenger seat, the amount of time my father always waits for the truck to warm up. I bolt from the bathroom and take the stairs two at a time. I put one arm into the sleeve of my jacket and stick my toes into the tops of my boots. With the jacket hanging off my arm, I hobble to the truck, the laces of the boots dragging behind me. I open the door and climb up to the seat. My father looks at me once and then puts the truck into first.

"I just got my period," I say.

To get to the highway that leads south to Concord, my father and I have to drive through the town of Shepherd. Few cars are out, most not willing to risk the slick roads even though the town plow has been by. Because it's Christmas Eve day, all of the stores and some of the houses have Christmas lights on. They twinkle weakly in the bright sunshine. My eyes are slits in the glare.

"Are you all right?" my father asks.

"I'm fine," I say, stabbing my feet into my boots.

"You need to stop at a store or something?"

"No, I'm okay," I say quickly.

I can almost hear my father searching for the right words to say to his daughter. In the last hour I've berated him, I've made him sad, I've chastised him, I've made him angry. And now I've given him this startling piece of information with no forethought and no preparation. My news has left him speechless.

"Will he talk to you?" I ask in the truck when we hit Route 89.

"I think so," my father says.

"Will they send her to jail?" I ask.

"If she's convicted, she'll probably go to jail."

"What will the charges be?"

"I don't know, really. Reckless abandonment? Endangering a child's welfare?"

He doesn't say, *Attempted murder.*

"It's all bad," I say.

"It's all bad," he agrees.

He drives slowly, his posture more alert than usual. The highway has only one lane open, which is slick in the shade, slushy in the sun. On the other side of the highway, traveling north, a car spins off the road into the median, creating a high tail of bright crystals that drift into the wind.

I sit forward, anxious and impatient. Will Charlotte still be at the station, or will she have been sent somewhere else? I'm hunched with my hands in my pockets. The truck's heater is pathetic.

Beside us, the snow rises ten, twelve feet in banks. Cars are buried in drifts and pine trees dip heavily toward the ground. When the snow melts or breaks apart, the boughs will snap upward, one by one, relieved of their burden.

"Will we be arrested?" I ask.

"I don't know."

We kept a criminal in our house. Warren will argue that we had ample opportunity to call the police, that it was our duty to do so. He as much as told us that already. And having not done it, we'll be found guilty.

"Are you scared?" I ask.

My father glances over at me and then back at the road. "You're a brave girl," he says. "Like your mother."

My eyes well up. I squeeze my hands together until my knuckles are white. *I won't cry,* I tell myself.

At the outskirts of the city, we take an exit off a second highway and find the street that the state police station is on. At the corner we pass the national guard building and then the Department of Transportation and the Supreme Court. My father makes a right and enters a parking lot behind a building that is large and square and modern and reminds me of the Regional.

"I'm going in with you," I say. I have the door open before my father stops the car. I'm ready to hop out at the slightest hesitation in his voice.

"You'll freeze out here," he concedes. He has on a brown knitted cap. Warren will think the man never shaves. The stains on his parka — that humpy, beige, shapeless jacket I'm so used to that it hardly registers anymore — are vivid in the bright sunshine.

I follow him along a shoveled path and into the police station.

My father frowns. We seem to be in the motor vehicles department. He checks the address he's written on a slip of paper. He asks a clerk where he might find Detective Warren. "That elevator there," the man says, pointing. "Third floor."

We take the elevator up. The floor is wet, and the elevator smells of cigarettes. On the third floor we find only a series of polished corridors, a row of wooden doors. My father sticks his head inside one of them and asks for Detective Warren.

"Oh," a young woman says. "You want the basement."

My father looks puzzled.

"Wait a second," she says. "I'll take you there," she says.

The woman has on a turtleneck sweater, a woolen skirt, and black boots. "Quite a storm," she says on the elevator.

In the basement she steps out of the elevator, holds it open, and points down a corridor. "The interrogation rooms and polygraph room are down there. That's probably where Detective Warren is. You actually can't go in that area, but over there is a cafeteria. If you ask someone, they'll tell Detective Warren you're here."

"Thanks," my father says.

The cafeteria has brick walls and fluorescent lights. Most

of the white Formica tables are empty. My father points to a black plastic chair. "Wait here," he says.

My father walks over to another table and asks a man in uniform how he might find Detective Warren. He gives his name. *Robert Dillon.* Hearing it always sends a small jolt through me, a reminder that he is someone other than *my father* or *Dad.* He is told to take a seat.

My father returns to our table and sits across from me. A middle-aged couple at the table next to us have their bodies turned toward each other. They speak in soft, coded messages. The woman says, *The third,* and a minute later the man says, *Only eighteen.* The woman says, *But how will . . . ?,* and the man says, *Walk.*

Detective Warren appears at the doorway.

"Dad," I say, and point.

My father stands. "I'll be right back," he says. "Here's some money. There are machines over there, or you can get a sandwich."

I watch my father walk past the detective. Warren's eyes are steady, his mouth firm. He gives no indication that he's ever met my father. Just before he turns to follow him, the detective glances at me. He doesn't smile.

I don't know what is said in the small room to which Warren leads my father. I'm not there. Later I'll be able to put some of it together from bits of conversation my father will recall. There's a two-way mirror and a tape recorder on a table. My father is not offered a cup of coffee

or a glass of water. He is told to take his jacket off. He sees
no sign of Charlotte, then or later.

He is asked to tell the whole story from the beginning.

From when we found the baby? my father asks.

Right from the beginning, Warren says.

My father tells the story of finding the baby in the sleeping bag. He relates it slowly and carefully, trying to
remember all the details.

Had you ever met Charlotte Thiel before that night? Warren asks.

No, my father says.

You'd never seen her before?

No.

My father says he first met Charlotte in our back hallway when she arrived in the blue Malibu. She said she
wanted a present for her parents for Christmas, a story
that, now that my father looks back on it, seemed thin to
him even at the time. He remembers the way Charlotte
later confessed that she hadn't come to buy something; she
simply wanted to see my father.

Why? Warren asks.

To thank me, my father says.

Thank you?

Yes.

For what?

For finding the baby. My father thinks a minute. *She also
wanted me to take her to the place where we found the baby.*

In the woods?

Yes.

Did you take her?

No. Well, yes. I didn't, but Nicky . . . started out. The next day.

My father explains that he wanted Charlotte to leave at once. *Actually, she tried to leave,* my father says.

He tells Warren about Charlotte fainting.

He tells of feeding Charlotte, of letting her sleep.

Of not wanting to know more than he had to.

Of Charlotte tripping over the sleeping bag. Bruising her palms.

He tells the story of her story.

Let me get this straight, Warren says, hitching his chair forward. *She told you that James said the baby was in the car. No last name?*

No.

And that when she got to the car, she touched the baby?

No, she touched the mound of blankets. She thought the baby was in them.

She didn't suspect a thing.

No.

And you believed her?

I did, yes.

What my father doesn't know, and will not learn until later, is that Warren has already heard this story. My father's version — apart from the possibility it might reveal new facts — is a way to check the consistency of Charlotte's confession.

Are you going to arrest me? my father asks.

We'll get to that when we get to it.

My daughter had nothing to do with this, my father announces.

I thought you said Nicky tried to take Charlotte Thiel to the spot in the woods.

Well, yes.

What happened there?

Nothing. I discovered they were missing and overtook them before they'd gotten to the place.

Someone's been there, Warren says. *Messed it up pretty badly, too.*

My father realizes his mistake at once. He doesn't know that Charlotte has already confessed, but he thinks that she might in the future. And he has no idea what went on inside the orange tape.

I had the distinct impression they were traveling away from the house and not returning to it, my father says in a halfhearted attempt to recover his credibility and to protect me.

But he is no match for Warren.

Why didn't you call the police? the detective asks.

I knew if I picked up the phone, she'd leave.

But you wanted her to leave.

Well, yes. But she was sick. She wasn't well.

Why not call an ambulance?

I didn't think an ambulance could make it up the drive.

I made it up the drive.

My father pauses. *Is this the point when I need to call a lawyer?* he asks.

Warren ignores the question. *She was leaving your house this morning for good,* he says.

Yes.

Where was she going?

I don't know.

You didn't ask?

No.

Why?

I didn't want to know.

A teenage boy is brought into the cafeteria and delivered to the middle-aged parents sitting next to me. The son is sullen, and the father seems nervous to see him in the flesh. The son will be released to the parents, an officer says, but he has to return that afternoon for the arraignment. I watch the threesome leave the cafeteria, the bewildered parents shuffling behind their boy.

I get up and walk over to the vending machines. There's one with soft drinks, one with candy. I select a Coke and a bag of M&M's and return to my table.

I finish the Coke and the candy. The officer in uniform gets up to leave. I think about getting some Fritos. After forty-five minutes I begin to worry. What if they arrest my father and forget to tell me about it? How will I get home? Who will pick up my grandmother at the airport? Will my father have to spend Christmas in jail?

Did she tell you anything else about the boyfriend?

That he was at school with her. That he played hockey. His parents live outside Boston. She says she called his family house, and his mother told her he'd gone skiing.

Incredible, Warren says.

Incredible, my father repeats in a rare moment of camaraderie.

My cramps, I realize, have disappeared. The Motrin is a miracle. I wonder if I need another pad. How do you tell? Do they sell them in the ladies' room, like they do at school? I still have some change left.

I leave the cafeteria and look for a sign that says Restrooms. I find it and follow the arrows, wondering as I go which closed door my father is behind. I listen for voices. I find the ladies' room. No one could miss it. It has the biggest symbol of a woman on the door I have ever seen.

When I return to the cafeteria, I'm disappointed not to see my father waiting for me. What if he came while I was away? I see a man in a suit in a corner with a cup of coffee and a newspaper. I take a deep breath and walk to where he is sitting. "Excuse me?" I ask.

"Yes?" he asks, looking up.

"Do you work here?"

"I do," he says.

"I'm just wondering," I say. "My dad went somewhere with Detective Warren?"

"Well, he's probably still with Detective Warren," the man says.

"He won't, like, have to leave without me, will he?" I ask.

"No, I'm sure someone will be out to talk to you."

It is not a reassuring answer, but I can see I'm not going to get a better one.

"Thanks," I say.

What happened after Charlotte and James got into the car? Warren asks.

They drove home.

And then what?

She said she wanted to bring the baby in herself, but he said he wanted to get her — Charlotte — in first, and then he'd bring the baby in. She did go in. She said she drifted off, because when she woke up, James was sitting across from her and he was crying.

And then what?

He told her the baby was dead.

And did you believe her, that a new mother would walk into a house and leave her baby in a basket in the backseat of a car?

Under those circumstances, I felt it was possible. Yes, I felt that she was telling the truth.

Why didn't you call the police?

Warren has asked this question before. My father's chest tightens. *I've explained that.*

Warren folds his hands on the table. *She was with you, what, forty-eight hours? At any minute during that time, you could have picked up the telephone. That's a lot of minutes to decide not to call the police.*

My father remains silent.

I could put you away for a year, six months anyway. Who would take care of your daughter?

Don't threaten me, my father says, standing.

Sit down, Mr. Dillon. Why didn't you pick up the phone?

I told you, he says. *I wanted her to leave immediately. When she sensed I wasn't going to take her to the place . . . in the woods . . . she said she was leaving. But then she fainted. I was worried. I said I'd call an ambulance, but she grabbed onto my arm. She said that if she went to the hospital, they — you — would arrest her. Which was true.*

And? Warren says.

And I couldn't force the woman into the car. She wasn't going to go willingly. On the other hand, I didn't want her leaving the house because she might faint again.

So why didn't you call the police? Warren asks for the third time.

What is this?

Tell me why you didn't pick up the phone.

I'm done here, my father says. *I'm leaving.*

What else? Warren asks.

What else? I don't know what you want. I remember thinking, If I take this woman to the hospital — assuming I can get her in my truck — it won't be long before the police hear about the postpartum patient and the old beat-up truck she arrived in. And I'd be more implicated than I already was. Which, to be truthful, didn't trouble me all that much. No, what troubled me was Nicky. If I were to be detained, or, worse, arrested, what was going to happen to her? Every decision I make now includes her.

My father leans toward Warren. *And there's something else,* he says. *My daughter watches everything I do. She counts on me to do the right thing. It was possible Charlotte was innocent. I didn't pick up the phone. I waited. And the longer I waited, the more complicated it got.*

Warren continues to stare. My father has the distinct sense that he is setting his own court date, but still he feels the pressure to explain — to himself now, if to no one else.

I wasn't willing to just walk away from her, my father says. *To leave her to you, if you want to know the truth. Every time I thought about picking up that phone, a bad taste would rise in my throat.*

My father stands up from the table again. He zips up his jacket.

She gave up the guy, Warren says.

The news startles my father. *You've already talked to her?*

He's in Switzerland.
She's already told you the whole story?
Skiing, Warren says.

The detective and my father appear at the entrance of the cafeteria. I jump up when I see them. "It's all right," my father says.

"What about Charlotte?" I ask.

"She'll be arraigned," Warren says, "and then a court date will be set."

"Can I go in and see her?" I ask.

"That's not possible," Warren says. He turns to my father. "Look, I've got some things I have to take care of, but you said you were going to be around."

"Yes."

"I may need to speak with you again."

"How did you know to be at the house this morning?" my father asks.

Warren jiggles the change in his trouser pockets. "The owner of the hardware store said he'd seen only three new people in the store in the last day — a couple from New York and a woman asking where she could buy a table."

The detective glances my way. He doesn't mention that the reason he might have questioned Sweetser a second time was that I said the Kotex wasn't for me, or that I lied about my father and the ax, or that a house far from town, dependent upon a well, might need electricity to power a pump to provide enough water for a shower during a power outage.

"It's why the plow came so early," my father says.

"Took all that time to get to your road. We'd just pulled up when we saw the Malibu."

"It's sad," my father says.

"They're all sad," Warren says.

My father and I go out into the bright light. My father puts on his sunglasses. I hold up my hand to shade my eyes.

"What happened?" I ask.

"He asked me a lot of questions."

"Did they have a two-way mirror?"

"Yes."

"Did they have a bright light overhead?"

"It was just an ordinary room with a table and a couple of chairs."

"And all you did was *talk?*"

"More or less," my father says. He looks at me. "Why? What did you think was going to happen?"

"I don't know," I say. "Something."

We climb into the frigid truck. My father starts the engine and backs the truck out of the parking space. He merges cautiously into traffic. He pulls too late into the right-hand lane and cuts a driver off. The driver honks his horn, but my father seems not to hear it. His movements are slow, his eyes glassy. He stops at a red light.

"Do you think we'll ever see Charlotte again?" I ask.

"I don't know," my father says.

The light changes but my father doesn't move. The car behind us honks again. "The light's green," I say.

We leave the city of Concord, my father driving like a senior citizen, to go back to our remote house at the edge of the woods. My father is lost in thought or replaying scenes in his head or thinking about what Detective Warren once said about needing to return to the places that moved us. I watch the road the way you might with a driver who seems likely to fall asleep. Both lanes are open, and the traffic is moving at a good clip. It is Christmas Eve, and everyone has somewhere to be.

We drive through town on our way home from Concord. I no longer have to tell my father to pay attention to the lights. He stops in front of Remy's and says he has to get a few items on Grammie's list. Each year, my grandmother calls ahead to tell my father what ingredients she'll need for the Christmas Eve meal. When she arrives she hits the ground cooking.

I wait in the truck for the six or seven minutes it takes my father to find what he needs. He's the fastest shopper in southern New Hampshire. I still have sleep on my face and I need a shower. I haven't brushed my teeth since breakfast the day before. But I am content to sit in the truck, my feet upon the dash, and watch people scurry to Remy's or to Sweetser's or to the basement of the church where the Congregationalists are holding their annual

Day-Before-Christmas Fair. Even men are taking baby steps on the slippery sidewalk, holding their arms out for balance. I see Mrs. Kelly, the mother of my friend Roger, on her way to the post office. I see Mrs. Trisk, my Spanish teacher, and I take my feet off the dash. My father comes out of Remy's, paper bag in hand, the minor miracle of a newspaper sticking out of the top. He sets the groceries on the seat between us and tosses me a devil's food whoopie pie. Muriel's sister makes them in the mornings, and they're usually gone by ten a.m. My father unwraps one for himself and bites into it as he backs the truck into traffic.

"Can we visit Charlotte in jail?" I ask, licking the cream that has squished out the sides of the pie.

"We'll try," my father says.

"Can I bring her the necklace?"

"I don't know the rules."

We pass the three stately houses, Serenity Carpets, the fire department.

"Listen," my father says. "I'm going to tell you two rules that you must never break."

I stop all movement, my tongue attached to the whoopie pie as if frozen to it.

"Never have unprotected sex," he says, pausing a moment to let this sink in. "And never, ever get into a car with a driver who's been drinking, including yourself."

These rules are spoken in a stern parental voice. I'm positive that the word *sex* has never before been said between us.

I slip my tongue back into my mouth. What brought this on? I wonder. And then I get it. That my father has delivered this pronouncement less than three hours after I revealed I got my period cannot be coincidence.

In years to come, through all the noise, these are the two rules I will remember.

My father stares straight ahead, as if he hadn't said a word.

"Okay," I say in a small voice.

His face visibly relaxes. After a minute I dare to take another bite of the whoopie pie. When I'm finished, I glance out the window and see that something has happened to the snow. It has melted and then frozen again into fine crystals that sparkle on every surface. I lick my thumbs and forefingers, put them together, and make a clicking sound.

"What are you doing?" my father asks.

"I'm taking pictures," I say. "I've been doing it all day."

"What are you photographing?"

"Just the snow," I say. "The shapes it makes. The way it lies on things. Like trees. And fences. The way it twinkles. The way it looks like diamonds."

We pass the cottage with its evidence of boys. A sled is propped against the front porch. I notice a wreath on a door. I peer into the windows. I think I see a fireplace, though maybe I only imagine it. In the driveway at the side of the house, a small gray car is stuck. A woman is inside it, and with her is a boy who looks about eight years old. As we pass by I can hear the engine revving, the wheels spinning.

My father pulls to the side of the road and stops. He opens his door and steps down onto the road. His hands in his pockets, he walks to the gray car. I lean over the seats and roll down my father's window.

"Hello there," my father says.

"Hi," the woman says.

"Want a hand?"

"I backed up, and now my car is stuck," she says apologetically.

"Let me give it a try," my father says.

The woman gets out of the car. She has on a green parka, and her jeans are tucked into rubber boots that come almost to her knees. A navy knitted hat covers her hair. The boy gets out of the car, too.

We listen to my father rev and spin, rev and spin, until finally my father gets out of the car. "You have a shovel?" he asks.

"I don't want to put you out," the woman says, squinting into the sun.

"No trouble."

"Well . . . all right . . . thank you," she says haltingly.

She takes a step forward and puts out her hand. "I'm Leslie, by the way."

"Robert," my father says, shaking her hand. He turns and points to me in the truck, my cue to get out. "My daughter, Nicky."

"And this is Jake," the woman says, putting a hand on her son's shoulder.

I move to my father's side as the woman fetches the shovel from her garage.

My father accepts the shovel from the woman, who laughs a little when she hands it to him. Over my father's shoulder, I can see an older boy, maybe ten or eleven, looking out of a window.

Jake moves closer to me. "You're the one who found the baby," he says. He has a round face with a receding chin. Snot has frozen on his upper lip, and he's a candidate for braces. I notice that the top of his mitten is chewed through. Who would want to chew on yarn?

"My father and I did," I say.

"And it was alive?"

"She's still alive."

"It was a girl?" he asks.

"Yeah."

"And it didn't have a finger?"

"No, she had all her fingers," I say. "It's just that one finger froze, and they had to take it off."

"Yuck," he says.

"Yeah, well."

I peer into every window of the house, cataloging white ruffled curtains, a flowered print wallpaper, a roll of silver wrapping paper, a lamp in the shape of an airplane. I note that there's a fireplace after all. From where I'm standing, on a snowbank, I can see into the kitchen, its light still on. Someone has made a terrific mess on a table. There are bits of dough and a thin layer of flour, a crumpled bag of King Arthur. On the kitchen counter is an economy-sized bottle of orange soda and next to it a mug with a tea bag draped over it. On a door that might lead to a cellar or to a pantry is a Santa done in needlepoint.

"You want to make a snowman?" the boy asks.

"Sure," I say. "Why not?"

Jake and I step-fall, step-fall into the snow in opposite directions. I roll the bottom of the snowman while Jake rolls the top. We make jerky swaths across the front yard. I push my monster snowball to his more modest one. From time to time I glance up to see my father shoveling out the back wheels or taking a quick breather.

"All right," I say, "let's put your ball on top of mine."

The two of us struggle to get the snowman's middle onto its bottom. I roll another quick ball for the head. We gouge out eyes. "We need a carrot," I say. "And two stones."

"Mom," the boy yells, "do we have a carrot?"

"In the fridge," she says.

The boy heads for the house, and I follow, uninvited. I stomp my boots in the back hall, but Jake runs directly for the fridge, leaving small grids of snow across the floor.

The older boy I saw in the window and now a younger one, maybe six or seven, come to stand at the threshold of the kitchen. The older boy has on a Bruins shirt. The younger has thick glasses that make his eyes bug out.

"You live up the hill," the older boy says. "You found the baby."

"It had a frozen finger," Jake announces, slamming the vegetable drawer.

"I know, stupid," the older boy says.

The kitchen is painted yellow and is smaller than I imagined. A jar of jelly with a knife sticking out of it sits beside a toaster. A box of Cocoa Puffs is on the floor. I see what the mess on the table was for: two plates of cookies, snug in plastic wrap, are on top of the fridge.

"We need stones," Jake says.

"What for?" the older boy asks.

"The eyes."

The older boy scans the kitchen. He settles upon a box of Whitman's. He tears the cellophane, lifts the lid, and reveals twelve dark round chocolates inside.

Perfect, I am thinking.

He passes the box around, and we each eat one. I take two and lay them on the palm of my hand. The boys put on jackets and boots. The older boy finds an extra hat and scarf for the snowman. "What's your name?" I ask.

"Jonah," he says. "And he's Jeremy," he adds, pointing to the little boy with glasses. They all look like the mother, with small upturned noses and wide cheekbones, though only Jonah and Jake are brunets. Jeremy has nearly white hair.

We dress up our snowman. The carrot and the chocolates give him a good-natured but dopey personality. When we're not looking, Jonah eats one of the eyes. Jake, furious and near tears, throws a hastily made snowball at his older brother. Instantly I am part of a snowball fight, though it's not clear whose side I am on.

"Boys," the mother calls wearily, as if she's said it fifty thousand times.

Jonah falls onto the snow and makes an angel with his arms. I can't resist and fall backwards, too. The snow gets up and under my jacket and my shirt. I remember that I just got my period and sit up. I'm too old for this, I think.

My father gets back into the car, guns the engine, and shoots forward. The woman named Leslie takes off her hat. Brown curls fall to her shoulder. Her bangs are stuck to her forehead. My father gets out of the car and says something. I can't hear what it is. The woman points toward the house, and I guess that she's inviting him inside for a cup of coffee or hot chocolate. My father looks at me and gestures toward the truck. *Groceries,* he must be saying to her. *My mother at the airport.* The woman smiles at my father, and I know she's thanking him profusely. He shakes his head. *It was nothing.*

"Nicky," he calls.

"See you," the boys say to me.

My father and I climb into the truck. I've got snow in my socks and down the waistband of my jeans. The woman waves us all the way to the turnoff.

"So," my father says.

While my father fetches my grandmother from the airport, I sort out the decorations for the tree. I'm working with the second-string ornaments. The box containing the "best" decorations is missing, and neither my father nor I know what happened to it. Among the ornaments we have left are six hand-painted wooden cutouts of snowmen. It's immediately obvious which ones I painted and which my mother did. There are five silver balls with fake jewels stuck to them, the result of another crafts project when I was eight. I remember the smell of the glue, the way the glitter fell onto the table, and how months later you could still see sparkles in the rug. There are a dozen small red wooden apples, most of them covered with a fine crackling from the changes in temperature in the attic. There's a paper plate with gold macaroni stuck to it and a picture of me at six in its center. My mother said it was the best present she got that year. Some of the ornaments have proper hooks and some don't. I construct makeshift hangers out of paper clips. I pull silver pieces of last year's icicles from the strings of lights and plug in the lights to see if they work. They do, but they're a mess. Every year we say we're going to wind them carefully before we put them back in the box, but we never do. We just dump them in.

In the car my father tells my grandmother about finding the baby and about the detective and about Charlotte coming to our house. He tells her about his visit to the police station, about Charlotte's being in jail. My grandmother is shocked and a little frightened. My father must also tell her that I got my period, because when she comes in, she gives me the kind of hug I haven't had in a long time, with a little rocking back and forth. She has fragile white skin with spots on her cheeks and forehead. She smells like the lavender sachet she will put in my stocking. I think her teeth are false, but I don't know for sure. She's a good person to hug, because her body fills up all the empty spaces.

She hardly has her coat off before she's looking inside the cabinets and the fridge to see if my father has bought all the right ingredients for the Christmas Eve dinner. I can hear her ticking items off under her breath: *pearl onions; nutmeg; beef broth*. She has brought her own apron, her own potato peeler. She gives me the job of peeling the potatoes with the new peeler, which works so well I don't mind the chore. I keep the water running at a slow trickle from the tap because it makes the peeling and the cleaning easier. Beside me my grandmother is cutting the tough skin off the turnips. She has a blade that's about a foot long, the kind that might figure in a horror movie. She digs into the turnip with both hands on the back of the blade and pushes down. The knife makes a hard thwap against the cutting board. I'm surprised at the strength in her arms. From behind, my grandmother is one large mass with a small head of tight gray curls. From the side, she is almost pretty.

"I got my period," I say.

My grandmother sets the knife down and wipes her hands on her apron. She pretends she doesn't already know. She envelops me in her arms. I still have a peeler and a potato in my hands.

"How do you feel?" she asks, holding me at arm's length.

"Good," I say. "I had cramps, but I don't now."

"Do you have pads?"

I nod.

"Do you need any help?"

"I don't think so," I say.

She puts her fingers under my chin and raises my face to hers. "If you ever want to talk about anything, you just have to ask me. It's been a long time since I had any bother with that, but that doesn't mean I don't know all about what to do."

She gives me another hug, and I feel in her squeeze a reluctance to let me go.

"Grammie," I say after a time.

"What is it, sweetie?"

"Do you know what pfeffernusse is?"

While my grandmother cooks, my father and I go out into the woods to cut down a tree. I worry that we've waited too long; it's late afternoon, and the sun is about to set. We have hundreds of trees to choose from; the problem will be clearing away the snow around it so that we can bring it inside. We both carry shovels, and my father has an ax.

Neither one of us says a word the entire time we are in the woods. The silence seems perfectly natural and comfortable and doesn't register until later that night. We are on snowshoes, and I follow in his footsteps. I have a shovel in one hand, so I can't put my thumbs and forefingers together, but I'm clicking pictures all the same. Of pink snow crawling up the side of a tree. Of the tips of the pines, rust-colored, on fire. Of tiny arrowhead tracks that skitter around a bush. My father stops and shakes the branches of what looks like a pointed bush. He begins to brush away the snow from the lower branches. Where the snow is hardpacked, we dig with shovels. It doesn't take us very long to clear around the base of the tree. My father bends over and takes a few swings with the ax. The tree topples and we pull it from the snow. We lay it down. It's a skinny tree with a few bare spots, but it will do. My father picks up the heavy end, I the other, and we carry it back to the house.

The tree is too tall, so my father has to take it outside again to saw off six inches. Once we've screwed it into the stand, I step back and see that it's tilted. We work on it for a while, until my father finally decides to tie it to a doorknob so that it won't fall into the room. He sorts the lights and strings them on the tree while I lay the ornaments on the table.

I am tall enough this year to reach the top branches of the tree. I hang the ornaments in an orderly way, trying to put them equidistant from one another. My father leaves me to it and goes upstairs to have a shower. The tree has fat colored lights, the kind my father says he had in his childhood. Last year, Jo's tree had tiny white lights with silver balls and scarlet ribbons and looked like something on the cover of a magazine.

When I am done I step back to admire my creation. I admire it in the reflections from the three darkened windows. I call my grandmother in and make her admire it, too. I sit in my father's leather chair, trying to decide whether or not I should move the macaroni plate to hide a bare spot, when I suddenly remember Charlotte. In jail.

On Christmas Eve. I slap my hands over my face. She is in a cell. Her parents must know now about the baby. She might have to stay in jail for a very long time.

I lean my head back against the leather cushion and stare at the ceiling. I know that Charlotte will always be with me, that I will think about her every day. She will become one of my small cast of characters with whom I frequently speak, whose lives I daily have to imagine. There are four of them in my little playlet: my mother, who remains the same age she was when she died and who gives me bits of advice on how to handle my father; Clara, who is three and who is getting a Cabbage Patch doll for Christmas; Charlotte, who will do my hair and shop with me for clothes and be my friend; and also Baby Doris, who might be having a bottle now. Or a nap.

I sit for a few minutes. I decide to put all the presents under the tree. There aren't too many, but I notice my name on a few. In the morning I will give my father the mittens I made, my grandmother the necklace with the sculpted pendant. She'll make a fuss and exclaim, but I'm guessing she'll probably never wear the necklace once she leaves the house.

My grandmother asks me to set the table, which is still sticking halfway out of the kitchen. I arrange it as festively as I can, running an assortment of half-burned candles down the center. I'm trying to think of something we own that will work as napkin rings when I see a flash of lights in the driveway. The car comes to a stop, and the lights go out.

My father, who's been in the den enjoying the luxury of not having to cook, walks into the kitchen, removing his reading glasses as he does so. "Stay here," he says to me and my grandmother.

My grandmother comes to stand by my side. We hear a car door shut. A few seconds later I hear a man's voice.

Detective Warren steps inside the house.

This is it, I think.

I worry about my grandmother. About the dinner she has made. About the presents under the tree. Who will be here to open them?

"I know I've come at a bad time," Warren says.

"Come in," my father says, shutting the door.

Warren does a quick two-step on the mat. His navy coat is opened, and the scarf hangs loose. I am used to his face, but I wonder at its effect on my grandmother: the gravelly scars, the flap of skin.

"Nicky," Warren says.

"Hi," I say.

"This is my mother," my father says.

"How do you do?" Warren says to my grandmother. "I'm George Warren."

No *Detective.* No *state police.*

My grandmother, both hands on my shoulders, merely nods. If Warren wants to arrest me, he'll have to tear me from my grandmother's grip.

"You're about to eat," Warren says. "Smells great."

"What can I do for you?" my father asks.

"I know it's a terrible time — I've got to get home to my boys, too — but there's something I think you should see."

"Where?"

"Not too far from here."

"It can't wait?" my father asks.

"I think you should see this now," Warren says.

I see a look — a kind of truce? — pass between my father and the detective.

"How long will it take?" my father asks.

"Half an hour? Forty minutes?"

My grandmother lets go of my shoulders and slips her apron over her head. "Don't worry about dinner," she says to my father. "I have to go upstairs and unpack anyway." She folds the apron and sets it on a chair.

My father takes his jacket from a hook.

"I think Nicky should come with us," Warren says.

My father climbs into the passenger seat; I slip in back. Warren makes the turn and heads down the hill. I notice there's a Snickers bar tucked into the backseat pocket.

"Charlotte Thiel's brother came and posted bail," Warren says as the Jeep bounces over the ruts. "Problem is, she can't leave the state. She's gone to stay with an aunt for the time being."

"Until the trial," my father says.

"Or until she pleads."

"What will the sentence be?" my father asks.

Warren makes the turn onto the road that leads into town. "Depends on James Lamont, whether he helps her out or not. Depends on Lamont's lawyer. Three years maybe? Worst case, she'll be out in fifteen months."

"And Lamont? Where is he?"

"His parents went to Switzerland to get him and bring him back. Now, him — he's looking at some serious time. Ten, twelve years. Might get out in six. The jury won't like it that he fled the country. And he can kiss bail good-bye."

"Does Charlotte have a lawyer?" my father asks.

"Her brother is taking care of that."

I wonder what Charlotte's brother looks like. What happened when they first saw each other? Did they embrace, a family in crisis? Or was he horrified? Furious? Struck dumb?

"Where does the aunt live?" my father asks.

"Manchester," Warren says. "I can get you the address."

"Please," my father says.

Thank you, Dad.

I will send Charlotte the necklace, I decide. I will tell

her that I got my period right after she left us. When she gets out of jail, she will call me.

We leave the village of Shepherd and travel on Route 89. The roads are completely clear. After twenty minutes or so, Warren slows at an exit and takes a right off the ramp. Immediately we are in a vaguely familiar town, one my father and I might have driven through during our aimless journeys in the summer.

We pass through a small village, mostly dark but for a Shell station on a corner. For a few blocks the streetlights have wreaths on them. I wonder what time it is: five o'clock? six? Warren takes a left and a right and travels up a hill into a neighborhood. I peer into the houses as we go. We pass a house with dozens of cars parked outside. Through the windows I can see men in jackets and women in dresses holding drinks. A party. A party would be fun, I think.

Warren looks at a piece of paper with an address on it and makes another turn. We are on a street lined with smallish two-story houses. Some have spotlights on their doors; others have lights along the rooflines and in the windows. One is completely dark but for a single blue bulb in each window. The effect is cold and unearthly. The road is plowed but still white. Snow is banked high on both sides. I'm counting Christmas trees as we go.

Warren studies the numbers on the houses. He slows the Jeep and pulls to the curb at the corner. He rolls down his window and peers into a house. "This should be it," he says, pointing.

It's a two-story house with a sloping roof and a room sticking out the side nearest us. The room has a lot of windows and might be considered a porch. The owners must have decided to use the porch as a dining room, however, because a number of people are sitting around a large oval table.

I roll my window down, too, and cold air rushes into the truck. "I got the address about an hour ago," Warren says. "Wanted to see the place for myself. It looks like we got lucky."

The table is well lit from a chandelier overhead. I spot a turkey, red flowers, white bowls of food. I count half a dozen kids, at least that many adults. There's an old woman at one end of the table, a man at the other. A boy reaches for a pitcher. A woman is walking back and forth under the archway of the wide opening from the dining room to the rest of the house. She's holding a baby against her shoulder.

I take a quick glance at my father.

The baby is wrapped in a white blanket that reveals only a tiny face, spiky black hair. The woman paces with a little jounce in her step, as if she is trying to get the baby to fall asleep or to burp her. She laughs and says something to a man at the table. The baby bobs her head and buries her face in the woman's shoulder. Almost absentmindedly, the woman gives the top of the baby's head a kiss.

"This is a foster home," Warren says. "The baby will almost certainly be adopted. White baby. Infant. But this is a good place to be for now. Some of them aren't so good, but this is a good one. After this I won't know where she's gone. It's why I wanted you to see her now."

My father is still, as if watching a critical scene in a film, a scene that makes you hold your breath. I know that he is thinking about Clara, and that there is, inside of him, an immense pain. But there is, too, a kind of healing, the equivalent of a sigh released. Through a lighted window we watch Baby Doris, whose real name we will never know.

After a time my father turns. "You ready?" he asks.

I try to speak. I shake my head.

My father nods, and Warren knows to put the Jeep in gear.

Acknowledgments

I would like to thank the wonderful Ginger Barber —
agent, confidante, good friend.

About the Author

Anita Shreve is the author of the acclaimed novels *Eden Close, Strange Fits of Passion, Where or When, Resistance, The Weight of Water, The Pilot's Wife, Fortune's Rocks, The Last Time They Met, Sea Glass,* and *All He Ever Wanted.* She lives in Massachusetts.